I0713669

Myths in Isolation

Katherine Soutar

ORKNEYOLOGY
PRESS

Published by Orkneyology Press

Stromness, Orkney Islands
www.orkneyology.com

ISBNs:

978-1-915075-22-2 hardback

978-1-915075-23-9 paperback

978-1-915075-24-6 ebook

Book sales:

https://shop.orkneyology.com/collections/orkneyology-press-books

Text © 2025 by authors as named in Acknowledgements

Images © 2025 Katherine Soutar

All rights reserved.

No part of this book may be used or reproduced in any manner for the purpose of training artificial intelligence technologies or systems.

The contents of this book may not be reproduced in any form without written permission from the publishers, except for short extracts for quotations or review.

Contents

Acknowledgements	VIII
Introduction	XI
Askafroa Cara Viola	3
Brownie Louise Norgate	9
Centaur April Madden	15
Dragon Janet Dowling	21
Erlkönig Jane Stemp	25
Fei Lian's Wings Liu Hong Cannon	31

Griffin
Fiona Angwin
37

Hippocamp
Jane Stemp
45

Imp
Jane Stemp
51

Jackalope
Janet Dowling
57

Kelpie
Jane Stemp
63

Laume's Lament
Georgë Kear
69

Melusine
Maria Gillen
75

Nekomata ~ Counting the Cat Tails
Nimue Brown
83

Otso and the Silver Child
Suzi Clark
87

Phoenix
Jane Stemp
93

Questing Beast
Jane Stemp
99

Rainbow Crow
Louise Norgate
103

Selkie and the Moon   109
Tom Muir

Tiangou ~ the Story of Chang Er   117
Suzi Clark

Unicorns   121
Bill Caddick

Vampire   125
Louise Gabriel

Wretch   129
Peter Stuart Lakanen

Xochiquetzal   135
Ursula Jeffries

Yeti   141
Simon Heywood

Zlatorog   147
Jane Stemp

Acknowledgements

The publishers would like to give our great thanks to the authors of these beautiful stories. Inspired by Katherine's gorgeous images, most were written especially to be included in this book. We thank you so very much for sharing your gifts with us all.

~ Tom and Rhonda Muir

The stories are credited as follows:

Askafroa - *first published in The Dawntreader 55* - Cara Viola

Brownie; Rainbow Crow – Louise Norgate

Centaur – April Madden

Dragon; Jackalope – Janet Dowling

Erlkönig; Hippocamp; Imp; Kelpie; Phoenix; Questing Beast; Zlatorog - Jane Stemp

Fei Lian's Wings – Liu Hong Cannon

Griffin – Fiona Angwin

Laume's Lament – Georgë Kear

Melusine – Maria Gillen

Nekomata ~ Counting the Cat Tails – Nimue Brown

Otso and the Silver Child; Tiangou ~ the Story of Chang Erby – Suzi Clark

The Selkie and the Moon – Tom Muir

Unicorns – Bill Caddick

Vampire – Louise Gabriel

Wretch – Peter Stuart Lakanen

Xochiquetzal – Ursula Jeffries

Yeti – Simon Heywood

Introduction

This book would never have happened if the pandemic had not hit us in spring 2020.

I work primarily as a book illustrator and during that first UK Covid lockdown in 2020, all my freelance work had suddenly been put on hold, and like many of us I was struggling with anxiety and feeling rather uncertain and adrift as everything in my world suddenly seemed to have utterly changed.

I desperately needed a focus. To get back to drawing as a way of working through my feelings a friend suggested a daily drawing challenge, which was eventually to grow into this book. The idea of taking all these characters from world folklore and depicting them in isolation gave me a focus and a way to get my own feelings down on paper.

The idea was to follow the alphabet. I would search for a character from world mythology each day beginning with the next letter and draw it by the day's end. I found many characters of some letters to choose from and very few of others - X and Z were quite a challenge! - and was introduced to many myths and legends which were completely new to me along the way.

These images are of themselves but also very much of me. They express so much about how I felt on the day I drew them. Some are almost unfinished, some polished. Some are dark and brooding, some thoughtful, some hopeful, even celebratory, some sad.

It was Tom Muir of Orkneyology Press who first seriously suggested that perhaps they should have stories, and offered a beautiful one of his own - S for Selkie.

The stories reflect the images beautifully, as they were written especially for them, in a complete reversal of the way these things usually work. They have been written by sixteen different writers and storytellers - some well–known, some just starting out, all talented and very generous souls.

Their stories reflect the times we are all living through, but with the original folklore themes running through them like a bright thread that connects the old with the new. It's a book for our time and a book for all times, as all the best folktale books are.

I would like to dedicate this book to all the writers who generously gifted me these stories and especially to Fiona Angwin, who sadly died of Covid during 2020 and gave me the beautiful griffin story.

Askafroa

Cara Viola

It was late summer and the ash was in a strange mood. Askafroa stood alone on a hill with elbows as sharp as corners. She chewed on bark; she spat out leaves. In full leaf, she was completely hidden from sight. In winter, people sometimes glimpsed her from below, but they usually thought she was a particularly knobbly branch. In a way, of course, she was part of the ash, in the sense that she could not stray far. She, in contrast to her ash, spoke the language of humans. She, in contrast to her ash, was of value.

'If, however,' said the ash in her mind, 'one were to chop me down, for instance, you would die too.'

'Yes, yes.' Askafroa turned her head from the trunk and looked over the hill. A human was coming up the grassy incline. She walked slowly as if something weighed her down, but Askafroa could not see what she was carrying. A loose scarf fluttered around her neck and mouth. Askafroa watched her and felt the familiar mixture of joy and dread in her sap. She knew what this was about. It was always the same. They came once every hundred years.

The girl stopped as she rounded the pinnacle, to catch her breath and glance at the ash with fear in her eye. Then she walked towards the tree and stood in the mossy shade.

'Well,' Askafroa said in the tongue of the girl, 'what have you come for this time?'

The girl's face twitched at the words and Askafroa saw her hands clench. She admired the girl for not running away.

'They say,' the girl said in a voice that was calm and much deeper than Askafroa was expecting, 'they say that you know how to cure all ills and that people come to you in times of trouble.'

Askafroa laughed because, a hundred years later, she was still right.

'Well,' said the girl, 'is it true?'

'Did they also tell you' - and here Askafroa leaned forward so that the girl could see her face. The girl stepped back, as Askafroa knew she would - 'that I require payment for each request?'

The girl nodded. 'Nobody could remember what it was last time.'

They never can recall that part, Askafroa thought. She stared at the girl, her gaze wandering over the straggly hair, the pinched cheeks, the knees that stuck out at an angle.

'What's the problem?' Askafroa asked.

'There is a strange illness,' the girl began.

'Yes, yes,' Askafroa sang out. 'I know all about it.'

'Can you help?'

'Oh no, oh no no no. Not this time.'

The girl staggered as if she had been struck.

'Why?'

But Askafroa did not answer; she was observing the way the girl ran her tongue around the corners of her mouth.

'You hungry?'

The girl nodded.

Askafroa reached up into the bows of the ash and slid her hands into a recess in the bark.

'Why,' asked the girl, 'do you look so human?'

'Oh,' Askafroa laughed, 'I look the way you imagine me to.' She extracted her hand and held it out to the girl. In her palm sat a fledgling blue tit.

'Eat,' Askafroa said, but the girl did not move.

'Not to your taste, is it?'

Askafroa placed the bird back into the nest and moved her fingers across the trunk, humming. Then she reached between two forking branches and when she held out her hand this time, a pear sat gleaming in the centre.

'Is this a pear tree?'

'No, silly. Don't they teach you those things?'

But the girl was not listening; she had bitten into the fruit. Askafroa watched her closely, the way her mouth glistened with juice, her fingers grasping the yellow flesh. When the girl had finished eating, she looked up at Askafroa for more. So Askafroa reached up again and broke off a small twig with nine leaves. One by one, she plucked the leaves from the stem.

'The first nine people you meet will be cured of all ills.'

'What about the others?'

'Oh, they will die.'

'Is that the best you can do?' asked the girl with the pear's juice still gleaming on her lips.

'No, darling. Come here.'

Askafroa wrapped her long arms around the girl, who felt sharp twigs and knots of wood dig into her skin. But the girl kept very still and she felt a warmth spread through her, and then Askafroa released her. For a final time, Askafroa reached up into the ash and picked a single leaf.

'Make a tea with this leaf and all who drink it will be healed.'

'But come back,' Askafroa called after the girl, who had begun to skip down the hill, her scarf fluttering in the wind, the leaf tight in her hand. 'That is my payment: you must come back.'

The girl turned and waved, her smile bridging the gap between them.

Perhaps this time, thought Askafroa, they would not forget.

Brownie

Louise Norgate

IN A WARM, DARK corner tucked below the old wooden staircase of the farmhouse, Brownie sat with his knees drawn up almost to his chin, the pointed tips of his ears twitching in displeasure. He heard the cock crow for the third time, as he always did, but today he was of no mind to settle down and sleep as daylight crept in. Today was different.

Sweep, sweep, sweep.

The night had begun as usual. Brownie waited for the last of the candles to be snuffed, and for the creaks of the bedchamber floorboards to fall silent. Only when everything was still would he creep out from his corner below the staircase and take up the broom. *Sweep, sweep, sweep.* All around the cool stone floors, spick and span, every last stray piece of straw or crumb or seed. The broom was heavy and he was always glad to return it to its place at the end of the larder.

On the low sill opposite, lit by a wash of silver light from the fattening moon outside, were a small saucer with a glistening chunk of honeycomb and a tiny earthenware jug of cream. Brownie devoured them with a happy chuckle, these morsels left by the small people of the house.

They were kind, the small people. Sometimes if they woke at night he would hear them creeping to take a peek at him as he went about his business, and he would wink slyly before slipping back into the shadows. It didn't do to be seen too much. He remembered years back, before the small people came, when he had presented himself to the master after he took over the farm: the master had looked down, given him a nod and left him to go about his business, as was good and right. They understood each other.

Brownie finished his cream and honey then, full and content, sat for a while to warm himself in his chair by the stove, rocking gently. The old mistress, who had set it here for him when they came, had often spent time here in the evenings. He would hear her from his corner below the stairs, fingers clack, clack, clacking at her knitting, which always went faster when she sat in his chair, for well she had known that his presence brought good fortune to the place. He had been sorry when she took sick, for not even he could have prevented that, and for a long while after she was gone he had worked extra hard at nights to keep the place as she would have liked it. Of course, now the new mistress was here, things had changed around quite a bit, but Brownie was happy that the master had insisted his chair remain there by the stove. He missed the clacking of needles, though: the new mistress did not knit.

Warmed through, Brownie resumed his work. *Shine, shine, shine.* The windows were cleaned and buffed ready to let in the sunlight tomorrow. He worked his way around the farm as usual. *Churn, churn, churn* in the dairy, *scrub, scrub, scrub* in the laundry, scouring away the marks of the day's hard toil on the master's shirt and breeches. They were often left at night now, for the new mistress did not come to them straight away as the old mistress had. *Scrub, scrub, scrub.* And so it went, cleaning and tidying his way around as always with the moon and the hoot of owls for company. *Busy, busy, busy.*

The night's tasks completed as dawn crept nearer, a satisfied Brownie returned to the house just as the cock began to crow. *Done, done, done.* His small, hairy feet padded across his spick and span floor on the way back to his corner below the stairs. Then, as he sat and drew up his knees, he saw it.

Opposite him in his corner was a neatly folded garment in green felt. Gingerly he lifted it and shook it open, feeling the unfamiliar texture brushing against his hairy arms and legs. It was a hooded cape, the perfect size for his tiny frame. He stared at it in disbelief that turned fast to indignation. This must be her doing - the new mistress! Oh, he had seen how the unfinished tasks about the house had begun to increase since she came, how there had slowly been more for him to do. And now of all things, she sought to pay him - a proud Brownie who loved the master and the small people - for his work? To clothe him, as if he were a servant? *No, no, no!*

Drawing himself up to his fullest height, Brownie crept out of his corner with the cape and listened. It was still quiet, but he would not have long before the master's family began to rise.

He strode determinedly to the larder and began, knocking over the jugs of milk and cream. *Spill, spill, spill.* He threw his empty honey-saucer hard onto the tiled floor - *crash, crash, crash* - and danced a sack of flour around the kitchen, billowing white clouds and leaving tiny footprints across the table and the floor. *Fling, fling, fling.* He tipped and smeared and toppled his way around until the kitchen was a scene of chaos: only the chair by the stove remained untouched.

Then, surveying his handiwork, Brownie dusted himself down, put on the green cape and left the farm, never to be seen there again. *Gone, gone, gone.*

Centaur

April Madden

WELL, COME ALONG; BEGIN the lesson.

Poor Achilles never quite learned it, but you are a better student than him, hmm? You have memorised all the uses of yarrow, and the wandering paths of the predictable stars. It's time you tackled a more advanced subject. Let us proceed.

How does one earn a place in the heavens? Very few do. Only four of Chiron's students ever managed it. His own place in the skies is far more mutable. Is he Apollo's pharmakos-knowing friend Centaurus, or Artemis' bold hunting companion Sagittarius? Or is he the little wounded healer that now bears his name, the dark-knowing comet, friend and confidant to quiet moons, staggering loopily amid the roads of the Great Conjunction? It would be just like him to wander in and out of the planets' weaving dance and probe its inner patterning. Father could always be distracted by that which he didn't know, and for that, I choose to believe that it is the last of the three that is most truly him.

I digress; return to your work. Who are the four prize scholars, and what did they have in common that set them among the stars? Do not say they were all sons of Zeus; that is a facile answer, and not entirely true. Many were the children of Zeus, and few were the ones that ascended to the firmament. In any case, one of the twins was the son of a mortal man. We had great hopes for Achilles likewise, but he chose another immortality.

Well? Castor and Pollux, Herakles, Perseus; very good, very good. And what was it that set them apart from their peers, from bright Achilles and bold Jason, from bee-wise Aristaeus and book-learned Palamedes and all their many fellows? Ah. That is a harder question, is it not? Well, contemplate it; you are here to learn wisdom, not mere knowledge. Any fool can recite facts, and does, if given half a chance.

Once, when I was a colt, my father asked me, 'Carystus, who is the greatest of my students?' I was slow to answer and he was patient with me; I went out to kick my hooves in the summer dust and to torment my sisters - boys are annoying whether they are man or horse, and twice as irritating when they're both - and when I returned I still hadn't settled on one. Wild Dionysus was the first I offered - I thought a god would clearly outstrip his classmates just by dint of birth - but my father told me no, he was drunk and defiant and impatient; wanting always to be first even when he had not earned the place. Clever Odysseus, I suggested next, but again my father told me nay; he was a sneak and a schemer, a tattletale and a show-off, and he had the ear of a sly and haughty goddess. Aeneas, I pleaded finally; pious dutiful Aeneas, who always did what the gods told him was right. No imagination, my father said; he should have stayed with the Carthaginian woman, and their bright and tolerant empire would have endured unto the end of the Earth, which would have been considerably later than it's likely to be now... poor sad impressionable Aeneas. In his grief he allowed himself to be led by soothsayers, and you should always ask yourself what it is they want.

Boys don't like to be beaten, do not like to be wrong, but eventually I had to admit defeat: I did not know. I thought he would be angry; he could be harsh when a student had not done their work, had not lived up to their promise. But instead his face split into its rare wide horsey grin, his eyes lit like he was Apollo himself.

'Very good!' he said, happily. 'The first step is in understanding that we cannot know everything!'

Pay attention to this; you may find it relevant. It turned out that my father considered that he was his own best student. So many of the young men he educated, gods and heroes, thought that wisdom was the same as knowledge, and that both were finite things; that on the day Chiron said to them, 'Go forth, your time here is complete,' they had learned all that there was to learn, knew everything that there was to know. Far from becoming wise men they became hidebound, arrogant - think of boastful Nestor, who never offered advice without recounting how qualified he thought himself to give it - and intolerant. Spoiled Ajax, if told there was anything more he could cram into his oak-thick head, would have taken it as a slight and an insult and begun to scream and throw things. By contrast, my father's eager mind, far from being outraged by any lack of knowledge, quite literally found itself wanting, needing, hungry, for anything it did not already possess. His greatest joy was the discovery of something he knew nothing about and had, perforce, to learn. He would have adored gothic architecture, Arabic mathematics, alchemy and quantum physics; they would have kept him happily busy for decades.

Speaking of which, how are you getting on with your lesson, hmm? How does one earn a place in the heavens? You've heard a lot about how you don't, by now - hubris, artifice, egotism, pettiness, self-doubt, rigidity, wilful ignorance - but as my father always said, 'Decide no suit until you have heard both sides speak.' So before we meet again, consider Perseus and his descendant Herakles, consider the Dioscuri, consider Chiron himself, and most importantly, consider all the many who did not have the benefit of his teaching, and yet somehow still managed to win themselves a place among the stars. How did they avoid the pitfalls that beset so many of his students? What did they learn that so set them apart, and where, and how and from whom?

We do not teach everything here, you know.

Dragon

Janet Dowling

I RESTED FOR A thousand years beneath the mottled earth.

Tired and beleaguered, I fled to the cover and comfort of the only mother I know.

Deep in her recesses, I found a cave.

Surrounded myself with man's gold and bright crystals that gave a resonance in the dark

to comfort me.

Safe away from the arrows, slings, the swords and lances

that sought me out, sliced my skin and scales.

Finding no pleasure in fighting back. Asking only for peace and understanding

to share the prosperity of the land. But there was none

to comfort me.

For decades my wounds festered and slowly began to knit.

Each scar a memory of an encounter with a formidable foe

I only wanted to call friend. Driven out of my pleasant land

away from my own kind. Will I ever find them again

to comfort me?

Now the sun shines through to my shelter filling me with new energy.

I feel the rays course through my veins, opening up new opportunity.

My belly fills with the food of hope, of courage and forbearance.

To rise now and fill the skies, find new friends, forge new alliances

to comfort me.

Erlkönig

Jane Stemp

THE WEST DARKENED, THE east lightened with moonrise. He had ridden far and was tired, and his horse was weary too. If there had been a loving heart at home he would have ridden faster, but some things kill love, and theirs had died a year ago and a day.

The road through the woods ran on low ground here. To one side alder carr rose from dark waters, to the other were drier slopes of alder coppice and woodland. As the moon rose higher it cast long shadows towards the last gleam of sunset, where the trees themselves were shadowy against the sky.

All had been quiet except for the soft thud of the horse's hooves, but with the night came the wind, clawing the rider's neck with cold threads of memory, lifting the leaves at the road's edge as if someone else rode alongside him. The thin trail of mist above the water shivered and faded.

'Who rides so late through night and wind?'

A figure moved on the edge of his sight, but when he turned his head he saw only the trees and the shadows and the darkness. He set his face towards home again and rode on. The wind in the trees pulsed with the sound of waves breaking, a beating heart, someone beside him. He reined in.

'Who's there?'

'We have met before.'

The clouds scudded across the moon, across the sky between the trees. In the shift and glimmer of light stood a man, his brows like a crow's wings across his forehead, in his eyes a look that was a challenge and an invitation and something else besides.

'I've never seen you before.'

'No. You did not see me. Your son did.'

His heart seemed to clench and freeze within him. The last time he had ridden this road had been a year ago and a day.

'He saw what was not there. I told him so.'

'You were wrong. I was there.'

Behind him the trees swayed like dancers in a ring, gowned with fog and crowned with moonlight and faint stars. The rider narrowed his eyes, as if that might sharpen his vision, and it seemed to him that he saw other figures among the dancers, light of heart and fleet-footed, circling a flame. He could not be sure.

'Do you want to be with him again?'

'I would give anything, anything in the world to have him alive again.'

The memory of the weight of loss in his arms, at the end of the journey, was as cold and heavy as his heart.

'I do not ask so much.'

'What do you want? Why did you want him?'

Moonlight through the fleeting clouds glanced on a hard angle of brow and cheek, a scar or shadow quickly concealed, a mouth lifted at one corner in what was not quite a smile.

'Beauty. Life.'

The rider laughed, tipping his head back so that his throat showed pale.

'I have no beauty to give you.'

'All life is beautiful.'

He stilled in his horse's saddle, his throat choking on the words.

'And I did not give what you took last year. You took it, in spite all of my asking. Despite all my fears. You stole it.'

'The child was so alive. He was so beautiful.'

'He could have been so now, if you had let him alone!'

His memories were like the small clear pictures at the wrong end of a spyglass, of light and laughter and love, in the before times, before love died.

'Who are you?' he asked.

'I am the Alder King.'

He stepped back, and the lost kingship of uncounted years was in the sweep of his arm, that seemed to lift the curtain again on the ring of dancers among the trees.

'Will you not come and be with him again?'

'How do I know that you are telling me the truth?'

And yet his eyes would not leave one figure in the dance, one small figure that he seemed to recognise among the many, candle-bright in the darkness.

'How do you know what is truth until you see it?'

The figure danced, turned. Was it waving to him? The rider hesitated; dismounted. He ran the stirrup irons up the leathers, and knotted the reins at his horse's withers to keep them from being caught by branch or bramble. Then with a slap of one hand on its rump he sent it away. Uncertain at first, soon it was cantering towards its stable and the journey's end, on the path that now lay clear in the moonlight between ash trees on the one side and elm on the other.

'Where are you?'

'I am here.'

'Where must I go?'

'Follow the flame,' said the Alder King. 'Follow your desire.'

He followed, moving heavily, a grey blundering shadow like a moth between tree-trunks and glimmering wreaths of mist.

'Life, beauty. I crave them, and satisfy my craving, and find myself alone again. Always I am alone.'

The rider neither heard nor listened, but stumbled among the roots of alder and elder, following the fen fire, Irrlicht, the fool's light that leads a traveller astray from the path and into worse than darkness.

Fei Lian's Wings

Liu Hong Cannon

FEI LIAN CANNOT SLEEP. His newly grown wings, though folded, still prick as he tosses and turns. War cries also keep him awake, though they have died down a little now that it is night. The enemies are fierce, he knows that much, and are led by the famed Yellow Emperor; they also have the advantage of local knowledge, for the Central Plain is their land; Sheyou's tribe, for whom Fei Lian will fight tomorrow, is the invader.

Hearing sounds from the next tent, Fei Lian springs up from his makeshift bed. Moonlight shines brightly on the figure standing outside, and he catches the glint of a dragon skin sack on her slender shoulder; a sack which, like his own wings, she can never remove. Suddenly he becomes acutely aware of how inexperienced they both are. Becoming god and goddess at such young age is not without cost. They have sacrificed their childhoods.

She turns at his approach. 'Can't sleep either?'

He nods, then: 'Yaoji, are you sure about this?'

'I never eat my words.'

'It's not too late to change your mind. I am a Jiuli boy, and have no choice but to help Sheyou and my people, but you are different ...'

'I'd lose out to that dreadful Hanba if it hadn't been for you. Do you think I will ever forget it?'

She laughs, and stretches her long arms with the grace and strength of the goddess that she is, causing loud echoes of thunder in the distant sky: 'Just make sure you give me the right push, so I can do my best dance.'

Morning comes. Riding high on the wind Fei Lian whips up with his giant wings, Yaoji loops round and round, gleefully tipping out the contents of her sack. Whole rivers falls from it, the hissing vapour of the flood blurring the boundary between heaven and earth. The two have danced before, but never so wildly, or with such spectacular consequences.

But a dance is the last word the wronged inhabitants of the Central Plain use to describe the devastation caused by Fei Lian's hurricane and Yaoji's rainstorm: people and cattle drowned, huts blown apart, trees uprooted. The Yellow Emperor's army is completely destroyed. Carried away, the two are oblivious to everything except for the loud praises Sheyou's troop's give their god and goddess. They are having fun, for even though they are gods, they are still children.

A sudden hush falls. A dark shadow presses heavily down from above. The beautiful, bright green grass abruptly turning brown. Yaoji pauses her dance and meets cold, merciless eyes staring from deep, skeletal sockets. Yaoji draws a sharp breath in: 'Hanba! What are you doing here?'

'I am summoned by no other than the Yellow Emperor himself,' hisses Hanba. Dry leaves are her gown, and ash falls like sand from her bony feet as she paces along.

Yaoji steps back. 'What would a king of noble heart ask of you, the Drought Goddess?'

Hanba laughs. 'To defeat you two of course. You forgot he was my uncle when I was a mortal. It's good, don't you think, that we fight out what we couldn't finish up in heaven?'

A spat between two goddess can have deathly consequences here on earth, and Fei Lian hears also prayers of the prostrate Yellow Emperor, lamenting the loss of life and blaming himself for calling upon the help of this goddess - even as he surveys the scene of destruction. The old man's pleas fall on deaf ears: Yaoji chucks rivers after rivers down, until she floods the earth, only for Hanba to scorch the land dry. Corpses pile up, cries for mercy fill the air; Fei Lian shouts for the two to stop, but to no avail.

Soon Yaoji slows, unable to do the rain dance without Fei Lian's help; she pleads for a strong wind, but Fei Lian refuses.

'Do you want Hanba to win?'

'No,' Fei Lian keeps his wings tightly closed: 'but the people have suffered enough.'

'We can't afford to lose,' she shouts angrily. 'We'd be doomed to stay here on earth, forever!'

Fei Lian says quietly, 'You are right. We can't lose, but neither should we win; hurricanes and storms are not good for the people, you and I were human once.'

'If we don't win, Hanba will plague the earth with drought. Then what?'

The anguished cry of a young baby reaches them, lying next to its dying mother. Fei Lian makes up his mind, and goes to the Yellow Emperor.

'Summon the Drought Goddess back to heaven and ensure that she does not fight again with the Rain Goddess.'

The Yellow Emperor bows, keeping his eyes on the ground in respect. 'I will obey you, Wind God Fei Lian; but how can I convince my people and the Drought Goddess that they will be safe from hurricanes and storms?'

Closing his eyes, Fei Lian starts to tear at his wings.

'What are you doing?' screams Yaoji, stunned.

'Making sure there will no longer be hurricanes and storms.'

'But without your wings you will never be able to return to heaven! And you have suffered so much and worked so hard to get them!'

'It's worth it,' says Fei Lian, bleeding from torn shoulders, 'for then there will be peace on earth and in heaven.'

Now he is a mortal, Fei Lian dies just as any other mortal would; he is buried with his wings. On the site of his tomb a temple is built, the most worshipped in all of China. Not long after his death the land becomes dry again, and as the Yellow Emperor comes to pray for rain, he sees Fei Lian, reunited with his wings, doing a gentle dance with his friend, the Rain Goddess Yaoji. The Yellow Emperor's prayer has been heard by the great Jade Emperor, who rules all Heaven; he has restored Fei Lian back to immortality.

Griffin

Fiona Angwin

THE GRIFFIN STARED AT his reflection in the water. The gentle ripples in the lake broke up his image and blurred the harsh lines of his cruel, curved beak. He thought it was appropriate, to be a little blurry. After all he was, in essence, neither one thing nor another. Humans always spoke of him with respect; he was both the King of the Birds and the King of the Beasts.

Of course, the humans hardly ever spoke to him. They were too afraid. Nobody spoke to him and that was the problem. Although he could trace his ancestry back to both eagles and lions, neither creatures saw him as one of their fellows. He was too - different. It hadn't bothered him when he was a cub ... fledgling ... hatchling. Well, not much anyway. He was a magnificent flying monster, the envy of all who beheld him. The trouble was, when he grew older he began to struggle. The two sides to his personality started to tear him apart. If he saw something or someone he wanted to chase and kill and eat, first he had to decide how to pursue it. Should he fly, and then drop down on its back from a great height, or chase it on all fours, loping along behind it and outrunning it with his powerful legs? Sometimes while he was making this decision the quarry would escape, leaving the griffin filled only with self-loathing, rather than supper.

He struggled to decide how to fill his time too. Should he spend his days soaring above the clouds? He could. Sometimes he did, but all the time he was flying, his beast side protested. Lions don't really do heights and that element of his body always wanted to have all four paws firmly on the ground; but when he was on the land his eagle aspect missed the freedom of the skies.

Basically he was thought to be one of the most mighty creatures on the planet, but he was both bored and miserable. He struggled with people's expectations too. Some humans - the braver ones - would climb up to his lair to ask for his help with some quest or enemy ... but for some reason they always expected him to be both magical and extraordinarily powerful. He was neither, and the disappointment in their eyes always unsettled him.

He turned away from the lake and prepared to take flight, to return to his lair at the top of the cliffs. He knew his basic problem was that his dual nature meant he was always lonely. He struggled to fit in. He had only been truly happy for the few centuries that he had shared his lair, and his life, with a mate. Those had been good years, when he'd felt he wasn't alone and had a companion to share his existence; when he hadn't feel like a misfit. Now she was dead, needlessly slain by some ruthless young man trying to prove he was a hero. Another reason to dislike humans.

He flew up to the cliffs and settled down into his lair. It was a cross between a massive twiggy nest at the edge of the cliff, and a den area in a large cave which opened onto the cliff edge. The two sections of his home were separated by only a strip of bare rock.

The griffin was about to close his eyes when he noticed something. There was a small red stone on the rocky area outside the cave entrance. A ruby. One of his rubies. One thing about griffins was that they were rather good at finding, collecting and hoarding stones - especially gemstones. His mate had loved the clear beauty of diamonds, while he preferred rubies and emeralds. What he liked most of all, once he'd collected them, was to hang onto them. Like many hoarders, he knew exactly where each of his treasures should be ... and that ruby should not be there. He stiffened. Someone had been here, uninvited.

His tail began to flick from side to side in annoyance. Suddenly he felt sharp needle–like pains. He spun round to find a small tabby kitten clinging to his tail, all of its claws sunk into his flesh. The griffin was raising a mighty paw to swat the little creature away when he was halted by a voice shouting at him.

'Stop! Don't hurt her.'

The griffin twisted his head around to see who was speaking to him. A young human boy of about thirteen was crouched in the entrance to the cave. He held a handful of the griffin's gemstone hoard in one hand and a short, stout stick in the other. He was waving the stick at the griffin in a way that made the massive creature want to laugh, but the boy looked so serious about protecting his kitten; the griffin attempted to look grave. He flicked his tail in the boy's direction, loosening the kitten, which flew through the air until it crashed into the boy, twisting round so that it could cling onto its young master. The griffin hid a smile as he saw the kitten's claws draw tiny drops of blood from the boy's chest. He was impressed to see that the boy was scared; he didn't look disappointed in the griffin now that he saw him face to face, or seem to expect anything magical. He didn't even seem to see him as a monster - just as an angry creature who had caught a thief.

'What are you doing in my cave?' asked the griffin with a lazy drawl.

The boy wasn't fooled into thinking that the griffin was relaxed about finding his home invaded. His explanation would have to be convincing if he was going to survive this encounter. He turned a variety of unlikely excuses over in his mind before deciding that for once, honesty might be the best policy.

'I am poor,' replied the boy. 'I have no home, nor food nor family, except for my kitten, Ra. And I heard that you had treasure which you never use, so I decided to take some of it.'

'Some of it?' queried the griffin sceptically, as he glared at jewels clutched in the boy's hand. 'It appears to me that you've taken half my hoard. Surely it wouldn't take as much as that to feed and clothe you ... or even to purchase a roof to cover your head?'

'No,' agreed the boy, 'but it took me hours to climb up here, so I thought I'd take as much as possible, to save me having to make the journey up here a second time when the money runs out.'

'It seems you are at least an honest thief,' said the griffin, amused. 'I'm glad you decided not to lie or I would have ripped you apart and eaten you ... although I must admit there doesn't appear to be much flesh on you. You're barely more than a snack.'

'As I said,' replied the boy, looking offended, 'I can't afford food.'

'You can now, it seems.' The griffin looked pointedly at the stones the boy held, and he reluctantly dropped them onto the ground. 'Better,' said the griffin, approvingly. 'What's your name, boy?'

'Just Boy,' he replied. 'I've lived on the streets for as long as I can remember. I must have had parents once ... I must have had a name, but I don't know what it was, and anyone ordering me around just calls me Boy.' He grinned and added, 'What's your name?'

The griffin blinked in surprise.

'No human has ever asked me that. They refer to me as Griffin - nothing more - nothing less.'

'Then we both need names,' said the boy.

'Indeed,' said the griffin. 'What name would you give me?'

The boy considered the creature then said, 'You are the King of the Birds and the King of the Beasts, so you need a name that suits both. I would call you Monarch ... but that's a bit formal. Perhaps you should be Rex? It still means king, but it's a name too.'

'Rex,' said the griffin, turning the word over in his mind. 'Yes. I shall accept that. You may call me Rex. In return for one jewel. Which I shall choose.'

It was the boy's turn to be surprised. It seemed he wasn't going to be a snack after all.

'And I shall call you ... Hatch ... short for Hatchling, since it's obvious that you are young. Will you accept the name?'

The boy nodded.

Rex settled down on his nest. The kitten crawled towards him and snuggled into his chest feathers. The griffin could feel the soft vibrations of its purrs.

'And what must I give you in return for my name?' Hatch had learned to be cautious, having been tricked and taken advantage of many times in his young life.

'I shall keep your kitten here with me for company,' said Rex.

The boy's face fell. The kitten was the only creature he cared about and he couldn't bear to part with her.

'Then I reject your offer - both the stone and the name,' said Hatch. 'Please just let us leave here alive.'

'You misunderstand, Hatchling,' said Rex. 'I am not swapping a gemstone for your kitten or your name. I am offering you both a home, here with me.'

'Why?' asked the boy, suspiciously. 'What's in it for you?'

'You may come and go as you please, sell some of my stones, so long as I chose which you may have. Some of them have sentimental value. Don't steal from me or lie to me and I will keep you both safe, in return for your company. That is all I ask.'

The boy considered the offer and found it acceptable, especially when Rex said that he would sometimes carry the boy up and down the cliffs on his back, for it was indeed a long and difficult climb. Hatch thought about having somewhere safe to sleep, money for food and of not being scared all the time. He thought about companionship. The idea of having someone he could talk to was wonderful. He was delighted to be offered a home.

Rex wasn't about to admit it to Hatch, but the boy had helped him to answer the question he had been struggling with. He had been so worried about which he was - Bird or Beast - that he had forgotten what he was - a living creature saddened by loneliness, a parent with an empty nest, an animal with the ability to give as well as take. He knew, of course, that eventually Hatch would grow up and move on to live his own life. Boys and kittens don't stay young forever ... but for now the griffin was content. He knew his own place in the world. He didn't have to be powerful or magical, he could just be kind. That was enough. For now, at least, he knew who he was.

Hippocamp

Jane Stemp

WHEN THE GODS OF the sea dance, the waves dance too. When the halcyon days come and the kingfishers nest, the waves glitter with sunlit laughter. And when the horses of the sea-gods, the hippocamps, came ashore in the evening to graze, the waves sang; but that was long ago.

Helike stood on the shores of the narrow sea, a city of pale stone with statues of bronze and marble, filled with men and women and children who led their lives as people do, through joy and sorrow, in beauty and ugliness and all that lies between. What they prized most in their city stood at the harbour wall: a bronze statue of the greatest of the sea-gods, his arm on the neck of a marble hippocamp.

A spring that rose far to the north ran in secret under the city and the statue; in its water was the magic and the gift of words. It flowed into the narrow sea, and so to all the seas of the world; and the words were those the waves sang in the evenings, when the hippocamps grazed.

One bright morning in winter, a ship came sailing out of the west towards Helike and tied up at the harbour wall. It was market day, and the people of Helike gathered round as the travellers came ashore.

'We are from Ionia,' they said. 'Our city is new, and we seek blessing and protection. Will you lend us your statue of the god, so that we may take it away and make another statue like it, and return it again?'

'How can we tell that you will return it?' the people of Helike said. 'And we, too, need blessing and protection.'

'Let us stay here,' said the Ionians, 'aboard our ship, until we have made the other statue. Then we will go away and trouble you no more.'

The people answered, 'Go away now, for you are trouble enough as it is. The statue is ours, and we paid its maker for it, more than it was worth. He promised us that there should never be another like it. Nor will there be, for he has gone away, so there is an end to the matter.'

The Ionians would have asked again, but the people shouted, 'No!' and some threw stones; so the Ionians untied their ship from the harbour wall and departed, rowing hard with the sails furled, since the wind was now against them.

Out to sea, beneath the waves, the sea-god and the hippocamp had heard it all, for the stream carried every word to them. The need of the travellers for blessing was sharp as pain, and the cold response of the people of Helike was a darker, deeper wound.

The day passed, and the night, and in the morning the sea-god said, 'This is beyond bearing. Skill of hands and words should be shared for a fair return. The statue is not a warrior, to guard Helike or its money.'

'What will you do?' asked the hippocamp, in a voice like the cry of sea-birds.

'I shall shout,' the god replied, 'and I shall stamp my feet, let come what will.'

When the greatest of the sea-gods shouts, the waves roar. When he stamps his feet, the earth quakes. Once, twice, three times he shouted and stamped his feet; and Helike, with its pale stone, its bronze and marble statues, with its grasping hands and cold hearts, slid beneath the sea and was overwhelmed forever.

When all was still again the hippocamp dived where the water darkened to green twilight, and with its sea-breath knew that the stream that brought the gift and the magic of words flowed no more. And it was sad, because it had loved that magic.

'Do not be sad,' said the god. 'I shall make the spring flow from the earth where it rises, and birds shall drink its water, and sing to you as they fly.' And he called to the winged horse Pegasus, who on the mountain called Helikon struck the ground with its hoof, so that the spring gushed out. Those who drink from it receive the gift of poetry, but since the fall of Helike the water is salt in human mouths, like tears, or like a memory of the sea.

Birds drank the water indeed, and sang whenever they flew near, but the sea was so strange now that the hippocamp could not be happy. At last it dived deep, and deeper, and swam under the earth where the stream had flowed, until it could swim no farther. There, coiled like a shell within a shell, it lay down to sleep, guarding the way to Helikon, as close as it could be to the magic and the gift of words, waiting for the time when it might flow to the sea again.

All this was very long ago, and the fishermen who used to tell how their nets snagged on the bronze trident of the sea-god's statue are long gone. But even now, when the waves break, white horses ride their crest; and when you hold a seashell to your ear, you can hear the waves sing, as they sang in the evening when the horses of the sea-gods grazed.

Imp

Jane Stemp

THE IMP PLAYED WITH the wind, hurling himself pell-mell from pinnacle to saint to drain-pipe, startling the pigeons as he leapt out at one level and disappeared into another, flipping his leathery bat-wings at the angels who never blinked, whose stone feathers never so much as quivered in the face of his small black joyful impudence.

Below in Minster Yard the scents of a discarded sandwich wrapper called to him - home-baked bread, real butter, bacon! - and he dived to snatch it from under the beak of a jackdaw no bigger than himself before soaring up and into the cathedral through the bell louvres. Back in his private nook over the ceiling of the Angel Choir, where two oak beams had been mortised into place nine hundred years ago, he curled himself into a knot of anticipation and sniffed, and sniffed, and sniffed, before licking the wrapper with his small, pink, forked tongue.

Evensong, it should be evensong now: that meant it was time to arm himself with pen and ink, and take up his place above the choir stalls. He was there to write down wrong notes from the choir and saucy talk from the listeners, to carry back to a lower authority proof of these small seeds of rebellion. Once, long ago, he had been perched above two gossips, writing so fast and frantically that he almost covered his parchment. Stretching it hard to make more space to write, he pulled it too far and it snapped, whipping him in the face and knocking him from his perch. A boy in the church, whom the townsfolk called simple but who could see where more complex folk were blind, saw the imp fall, and laughed out loud in the middle of the sermon. He was thrust out of doors to run in the sunshine, and the imp flew out to play with him instead of sitting while the dull words fell on stony ground. The boy had told his tale to a mason, and after that there were two imps in the cathedral, one made of stone.

A while and a while; still nobody came. The imp had only the vaguest sense of time; perhaps he had not heard all the chimes, or had made some other mistake. He sniffed the paper in his hands, which was still haunted by delicious ghosts of bacon and butter. With a bat–high squeak of glee he abandoned pen and ink and scrambled up into the roof–space, where he launched himself down the curves of limestone, tobogganing on the buttery paper and flying up in the nick of time from the great stone capitals where the vaulting sprang.

He came up from the most dizzying spiral of all, ready to turn and spin and fly again through the rippling space between vault and roof, only to find himself caught by the scruff of the neck and set down hard in front of two black, webbed feet. Above him was a vast swansdown bosom, and far above that a black-and-orange bill and two beady eyes.

'Such goings-on!' the swan said. 'And in this place, too. It's easy enough to tell which field you were raised in.'

The imp peered cautiously round the feathers and past the folded wings, rubbing his neck; even a spirit-swan has a ferociously hard beak.

'Is Hugh coming?'

'Saint Hugh to you, young impet.' She shook herself like an aunt settling a shawl across her back, and sat down.

The imp sniffed. 'Young? I remember you out of the egg, you overgrown duck. Smudge of grey fluff, tripping on your own feet.'

'Some of us get wiser with age,' the swan retorted. 'No, the master's not coming, not this time. But he'll be watching, today, along of the others. Now that they aren't here.'

He knew well enough who she meant. But - 'Not here? They're always here.'

'You come and look.'

Together they peered through the one place in all the forest of stone and wood from which you can see the length of the building and its height. The chairs had already been cleared away, and slowly, candle by candle and bulb by bulb, the lights were going out. Two vergers snuffed each flame, electric lights blinked dark with no warning. Twilight crept from west to east.

'What's to do?' the imp said, for once uncertain and a little alarmed.

'Plague,' said the swan portentously. 'They have to stay indoors, and not meet their friends for safety's sake, not till 'tis gone.' She settled her feathers again and said with withering scorn, 'I can see them doing that, ho I can, for sure. They won't wait, folk in this age. Want it all now, whether it's food or the latest fashion. Lads walking around like they own the earth, and lasses dressed to kill, or so they call it. All blush and no bonnet, I say.'

'You would', thought the imp, but said nothing. He felt sorry for them, who wanted everything now, and couldn't wait. Why, even a bacon sandwich was only as good as the time before you ate it, because then you ate it, and the lovely moment of anticipation was gone as well as the sandwich, and the only thing left was to want another one.

The two vergers walked out of the cathedral with slow and heavy footsteps; but not so slow or so heavy as the ticking of the tower clock. The door in the Galilee porch opened and closed, and the key rattled in it; then the door in the west front. This was not the great door, but a smaller one; still, it closed with a noise that made the stone and silence ring.

The swan and the imp looked at each other.

'What now?' asked the imp.

'We wait, of course.'

Through the west window came a dazzle of sunset light that flared as if it shone through moving feathers, and then a swirl of wind that knocked him backwards and over like a falling leaf until he remembered what his wings were for.

When he had recovered himself he flew back to his place above the choir. A little of the light crept in even there, reddening the darkness into warmth. He made himself comfortable, closed his eyes, and began to dream of bacon sandwiches.

Jackalope

Janet Dowling

AT THE BEGINNING OF time the creator stood back and marvelled at her work. Everything was as it should be, and everything was in its right place. She had created all the animals, and now on this day, she allowed them to make one request to change things. Most of the animals were quite happy with what they had been given but some wanted to be different. The first in line had been the jackrabbit.

'This tail is too long' he screeched. 'I keep tripping over it!'

The creator smiled. 'That's alright. I can see you like to run fast. It would probably be better if you have a short tail. Which one would you like?' She showed the jackrabbit the box of tails.

'I'll have this one,' he shrilled, pointing to a short tail.

'Well done,' said the creator, 'I couldn't have chosen better myself.'

The jackrabbit was pleased with himself. As he passed the queue, he made sure to twitch the tail every now and then to show it off.

'I got the very first exchange,' he squealed. 'The creator said she couldn't have chosen better.'

Then he sat back and watched as the queue got smaller, and the other animals showed off their own exchanges. When the antelope passed by Jackrabbit gasped. On the antelope's head was a magnificent set of horns. He watched as the antelope started to run across the plain with his head held high. Jackrabbit so wanted a pair of those.

The sun went down in the sky, and the moon rose. Creation day was over.

'Now,' thought the creator, 'time for a rest.'

She looked down at her collection of spare parts and decided that she would tidy up later. After all, there was no one else to please. But in front of her was a cloud of dust! It was Jackrabbit running as fast as he could.

'Please, please, please! May I have some horns? I'd really like some horns. Please. Please, Please.'

'I'm sorry,' said the creator, 'you've already have exchanged your tail. I'm trying to be fair to everyone - just one choice per animal.'

'Please,' said Jackrabbit. 'I was first in the queue. I didn't know what else was on offer.'

The creator looked down at Jackrabbit. He looked so doleful. And she really wanted a rest.

'Alright,' she said, 'but tell me what you want to exchange for it?'

Jackrabbit was startled. He had not thought what he might give up. He liked his new tail. He liked his legs. He liked his twitchy nose. He did not like his squeaky voice.

'My voice. I'll give up my voice.'

The creator looked at him.

'Are you sure?' she said, 'Won't you need to talk with other animals?'

Jackrabbit shook his head. He was determined to have the antlers.

'Very well, here are your horns.'

The creator reached down into the box and pulled out a pair. They had been very knocked about, but Jackrabbit didn't care. He had horns, and scurried off into the night feeling very proud. But he was no longer a jackrabbit like the other hares. They were very sad that he could only speak with a grunt. Nor could he join in their games because the horns were so sharp that he accidentally hurt them. They called him the Jackalope and shunned him. He was so sad he went out into the plains - far away from other animals and the hares.

But one other animal often travelled over the plains: Man with their cattle. Sometimes they would hunt the Jackalope and roast it for their dinner. The Jackalope didn't know what to do - when cornered they would fight furiously, and man would be covered in scars from the antlers. But that didn't stop them.

Then one night a Jackalope came across some men around a campfire. He froze, hoping that they would not see him. He wanted to warn his family but with no voice there was nothing that he could do. The creator looked down and saw the dilemma the Jackalope was in. She could not give him his voice back, but she could do something else. She summoned the wind. As the men talked in the night across the fire, the wind carried their voices to the Jackalope with his mouth open. As his mouth filled with their voices he tried to spit them out, but as he did the words themselves echoed back and around.

'What's that noise?' called out one of the men.

'What's that noise?' came the echo back from the Jackalope.

'Stop fooling around,' called another.

'Stop fooling around,' came the cry back.

The men counted around the circle - they were all there. Someone or something was out there.

In the dark they could not see anything. They staggered around trying to find the source of the echo, but as they came near to the Jackalope he rushed towards them, stabbing here and there with his horns. The cuts ran deep and the men rushed back to the campfire, convinced that they were being attacked by ghosts. They didn't sleep all night and when the dawn was up, they took the cattle and raced on their way. They began to tell the story of the haunted places where men were cut to pieces. It was told time and again.

Men avoided the area, but if they did camp there, the Jackalope knew their best defence was to hide, and then surround the camp at night. This time there was not one, not two but many voices reflecting back the words and the songs of the men. The men quaked in their boots. They did not know what spirits they disturbed, but they did know the price they had to pay. And that was too high.

And that is how the Jackalope is the king of the desert plains and man does not dare disturb them!

Kelpie

Jane Stemp

EACH DROP OF WATER from the overhanging branches fell into the stream with a noise like stone on stone, faint but clear through the smoke of mist that drifted over the ground. For all the still night there was an odd, chill breeze blowing. Ailie had been treading carefully, the basket at her hip heavy with butter from the kine and honey from the hive, gifts from Mistress MacPherson at Cuillean. She had stayed there all evening, for the old lady had been yearning for a young thing about the house, and had given her broth to sup and spring water to drink and spun long yarns of when she was a girl.

Now Ailie quickened her pace, mindful of the late hour and the folk waiting for her at home, and came out from under the trees to a place where the stream tumbled peat–brown over granite boulders into a pool. She slithered down the slope, recovered her balance and went on across the cropped turf, dew–bleached in the moonlight. The path curved to the right here, and as she followed it, something dark bulked in the corner of her eye. She stopped. No more movement, but it was still there. Ailie set her lips together and turned toward it. Better to see it than not to know.

It was like a horse, but it was not. There was a tale Mistress MacPherson had told her. She would have to pass between it and the water. Kelpie. Her lips formed the word, but no sound came, only a breath of air on the cold night that drifted before her eyes and was gone.

The thing had no visible substance; it might have been drawn in strokes of pallid light on the darkness. Each wild lock of its mane moved slowly like weed underwater. A shimmer of green danced and slid on each curve and plane of its face as if it, and she too, stood waiting in the depths of the stream.

Between the shifting outlines it was darker than the dark behind it. Ailie dared not move; but she had to move. The thing was not blocking her way. It drifted beside her, no closer, as she took one step, another, along the path between it and the water's brink. She edged away from it, and her foot slipped. She fell with the basket hugged close to her right side, and her left hand slapped down into grass that seemed coated with fine grit. She curled her head and shoulders down, for now surely the kelpie would come for her, and carry her off into the dark water.

There was no sound but her breath, and the damp shift of hooves that were not quite hooves on grass. Nothing else happened. Slowly she sat up, still hugging the basket close. The heel of her left hand stung; she licked at the graze, and tasted salt. But she was not bleeding. Wondering, she pinched a blade of grass between finger and finger, and wiped it clean. The fine grit was salt.

Ailie looked up, and saw the kelpie pacing a curve, like a caged animal in a zoo. It must have come out of the water, and someone had bound it in a circle of salt, and now it could not return to the stream. She was safe. Quite safe. She scrambled to her feet, and kilted up her skirts in her left hand to run away.

There were voices in the distance, borne uphill on the chill breeze. Lachlan, and Jamie, and the new hand from beyond Kessock whose name she could not remember. They were arguing as usual.

'A silver bullet, that will kill it and no mistake!'

'Why would we do such a thing, when we can bridle it with the sign of cross? Better a strong horse to do the heavy work that the laird lays on our backs.'

The kelpie whickered, a noise as if ice wept. Ailie could not help but turn around. It turned its head slowly and looked at her out of its left eye. Green and wild was the eye, and cold. But there was also a sadness that drew her deep in, and somewhere behind that a white figure that might have been a reflection of herself, or the ghost of a ghost or a long–ago dream; but whatever it was, it was human, or had been once. The wild and the dark water was the nature of it, and not of its choosing.

Ailie set down the basket and dropped to her knees again, scraping and tugging at the grass, leaning down to the stream to scoop up water and wash every blade clean for a space as wide across as her two arms could reach. Then she drew back, clutching the basket in front of her again, as if it would make a shield for her if need be.

She did not need it. The kelpie stepped daintily forward, head down, cautious, then found itself free, and in one leap, a surge of dark, it was gone, leaving behind it a swirl of cold air and a noise like distant thunder.

Ailie took the other path back, down the gentler slope where she would not meet the three men climbing up from the stream's fall into the millpond, and as she walked towards warmth and home she wept, the tears salt on her face. Not for herself, nor because of the fear that had passed, but for the creature that had gone back alone into the darkness of deep water.

Laume's Lament

Georgë Kear

WHAT IS IT?

Not who is it. But what is it ...

I may be stone. I may be thousands of years old but I remember. I am awakening like lightning splitting a cloud. My life changed and hardened and fossilized me. Now light, childish voices discuss me.

'Hello ...?'

Yes I remember children. They sound afraid but I'll not soothe that. Not just yet.

I was once weather. When elements were worshipped. I sat on a throne made from hailstones and ice crystals that glittered like diamonds, in a castle of swirling vapours, with curtains of clouds and doorways cut through by biting winds. I was larger then.

We were sky spirits who danced on thermals with the circling eagles and swooped with swallows and bats in the first and last lights.

I was promised to be married one Thursday to the God of Thunder. I saw him once, driving his chariot over the noon sun, pulled by miserable goats who should have been free to skip on the mountains below. But I was in love with moonlight and starlight and he seemed determinedly daylight.

Quietly I wove a ribbon in every colour I could find. Red and orange from sunsets. Yellow from the sun. Green from the young clouds who were astonished by the trees below. Blue from the sky. Indigo and violet from the beginning and end of twilight. It was a fine, wide ribbon, designed to be my escape to the moon, but I had unconsciously woven an arc, it curved downwards and I found myself on the ground.

Of all my sky sisters, I had been the only one to look down, hanging over the side of my diamond throne, sucking on snowflakes, my tears becoming rain as I saw earth children orphaned, abandoned, neglected, unable to play. I was Goddess of the Soft Heart; I have been scorned and derided for it. My reputation besmirched, my sweetness and gentleness mocked and ignored along with the other lionesses in history.

I learned to weave from my mother but no matter how hard I tried I could not weave them happy fates. The cloths seemed to create themselves, spreading happiness and sadness so randomly and unfairly that I became bewildered with the hopelessly tangled threads and broke my heart with weeping until my mother bid me stop in case the children drowned.

I have been down here for a long time now. I am most powerful under a new moon; both this moon and I are invisible to the unaided eye unless we have stars behind us to illuminate our outline of silver. I am weakest on a Thursday.

At first I was happy here. The lakes and dense forests were just as beautiful as my celestial castle. I could cause hail, rain and storms by singing and stamping my feet. When I danced I left faery circles in the grass in which mushrooms, toadstools and wildflowers sprang to violent, vivid life. I rejoiced in the cycles of the seasons. Snowdrops, bluebells, foxgloves, roses, falling leaves and pinecones, snowdrift flurries, then snowdrops again, dainty, brave, heralding warmer days.

The lakes carried icebergs in the winter. I would stand alone at the water's edge, the soft blue galleons reminding me of white clouds on which I had once slept, they enhanced my solitude with the melancholy happiness of memories that rolled across centuries.

Children knew me as a woodland fae and would visit, bringing little handmade gifts. Whenever an orphan was born or made, villagers would leave it in my faery ring and I would kiss its forehead to lessen the pain of loneliness and wrap it in leftover ribbon, crying a different, unconditional tear for each one, a silent guide for the rest of their lives.

I missed my sisters. There was nothing else on earth like me. The forest creatures, horses, goats, bears, wolves and birds became my friends. As I solidified from airborne thing to earthbound thing my beauty changed. My clear eyes carried clouds; I grew owl talons in place of feet and from my head sprang magnificent, curling horns. I slept on soft pine needles and began to notice that the children no longer came.

I knew when an orphan was made because I spoke to the trees who, with their roots in the ground, knew who was buried and who was not. But still the children did not come.

The world changed. People no longer spent time outdoors. They did not welcome the rain; they mistrusted the forest and kept the children indoors, telling them the only acceptable and safe things were between those four walls.

Without the moon above them or the poetry of things they could not explain my reputation changed. From a benevolent woodland fae who loved and suffered for all orphans, my sweetness and beauty was bent into ugly rumours of an evil baby-snatching hag who could not have children of her own. They threw iron at me, knowing it bit and stung, driving me further and further away.

Here in this hidden cave, I have been curled into a ball, creating the smallest possible shadow so it cannot be stolen. I am safe in this ring of candlelight, except for the rainbows that spit and curl out of my pretty horns, these are not safe; they give me away and are easily grasped and twisted off. Once these are taken I doubt I will continue to exist.

I am older than weather. I am older than magic. I have survived these times where we all became just one thing, instead of many free and far-ranging complexities inside one soul, different responses to each season, afraid of things that cannot be named.

Yet I have spent so much time deep in my dreams I am slow to react, my owl feet in treacle, my resentments hardened and fossilized inside me.

I may be stone. I may be thousands of years old but I remember. I am awakening like lightning splitting a cloud. I can still shapeshift. I can still cry tears of rain. You will find when you miss me that I have gone home.

As you pause in the doorway ask yourself just one thing: 'When I am abandoned, orphaned by life, a perpetual child, do I need someone to love me, guide me, weep for me and wrap me in rainbows?'

Yes, I remember children. They sound afraid but I'll not soothe that. Not yet.

'Hello ...?'

'What are you ...?'

Melusine

Maria Gillen

MÁIRE SAT AT HER desk in her business suit, an impressive figure typing away furiously. She seemed totally absorbed in her work - yet there was one corner of her mind playing in technicolour hovering over the deadlines and spreadsheet, gently tapping on her attention. If you could look inside her head, you would know she had to keep her mind busy - every time she stopped an ancient tune tapped at the corner of her mind and sepia memories splayed out on to her internal landscape.

She still lived in Granny's House - a childhood haven, but even here the sepia dreams and that damned tune invaded. Her mind strayed to how Granny would not be pleased if she could see her garden now.

She had worked hard for what she had - growing up with Granny there was never any spare money but always an embarrassment of wealth in love.

'Sure you can't take it with you girl.'

She brought her mind back to the project - concentrating on who was responsible and when it must be completed. This grounded her, she knew she was good at what she did. Yet lately she was not that measured, competent leader. She was the nervous wreck that heard strange music every time she closed her eyes.

That tune teased around the edges of consciousness. She found herself humming it now - when she woke up, when she was parking the car, while she awaited her turn to present at meetings. What was that tune?

She roared out loud now to the invisible forces that were haunting her. 'Right then, show me! Show me who you are and what you want of me! Show me or LEAVE ME ALONE!' Whew! But that felt good - her face flushed and her eyes dancing, she looked so much younger. She shouted out again - 'Show me or leave me alone!' This time the relief made her laugh out loud - and the music stopped ...

That night in a deep relaxed sepia dream she heard the tune again. This time she was in the memory. She was not observing now - she could feel the soft breeze and she could touch the hurdy gurdy looking into the laughing chocolate eyes of its owner - an old lady, definitely not her beloved Granny, but so similar she could be her sister. She pointed now, to the bottom of the massive, magnificent manicured gardens. Máire looked to the faraway place she was pointing to - then as it is in dreams she was floating in time to the ancient tune - down, down inside a circular brick structure. It was dark - but she felt the bricks were red, they were old and in places a gentle green moss grew (How did she know that? - yet she knew it as sure as she knew her name was Máire).

As natural as breathing, she floated under the cool water where her watery delighted giggles merged with the music of the familiar tune. The water was refreshing on her wide open eyes.

Máire's eyes were drawn like magnets to the figure coalescing in the starlit water. First her long fluid back, the back of her head slightly turned in profile and her hair floating up and out like a silky protective flower. Then her long tail - where legs should be, at first curled under her almost like the tail of a seahorse. She rose and with a delicate elegant movement of her hand the majestic ethereal tail unfurled. Máire felt a warming of her blood as she beheld the frothy delicate fronds - oh the magnificence of it. Would there be an artist in the world that could capture this beauty?

No need for words here - Máire called to her from that place somewhere between the heart and gut. The figure began to turn and Máire's arms stretched out in longing for an embrace.

'Mom, Mom, MMMOOOOOMMMM!' The urgent cries penetrated her dreams and her son, red faced and crying, called her back from her peaceful dream.

He was feverish and frightened - he had been sick all over his bed and his temperature was sky-high. She cleaned him first, taking off his soiled pyjamas, wiping him down with a lukewarm cloth, then putting a cold compress on his head.

At times like this he liked to wear one of her t-shirts - it had her smell. He had her husband's 'here before' eyes. Oh, how she missed him. Her beautiful man, her soulmate. Tears streaming now, she found herself crooning the haunting tune to her five-year-old and was mildly surprised that it soothed him. She put the soiled items in the washing machine and lost herself in her spreadsheets. She was delighted that she had gotten a march on the day, when her son came into the doorframe - holding his blankie, his eyes accusing.

'I was sick, Mommy, I was sick and you didn't stay with me.' Then he began to sob. 'I want my Dad!' he howled.

She was mesmerised at how Dónal remembered his Dad, and called on him. He had barely had two words when Adam had died.

'Now, now,' she crooned, but he could not be consoled.

Máire stalked the internet for an image to match her dream. When she found it, she saw that the artist was an exotic woman, with penetrating blue eyes and long silver hair. She looked so wise and Máire felt she was the type of person who had really experienced life. She had named her painting Melusine.

That night, deep in her dream her heart called out to the presence: 'Melusine!' The floating creature turned and smiled - pleased with Máire's efforts. Melusine sung in watery notes deep into Máire's heart and her spirit reverberated with recognition.

'I'm Melusine, Melusine

Please listen to me

I bring the water of life

Máirín, Máirín you know in this life

There's no need for trouble and strife.'

The song lifted her far above the water and well to an ariel view of Granny's Garden. The lawn was manicured with a few daisies smiling up at the moon. She could smell the night stock and see the big fat red roses bobbing a curtsy to her. She lay down on the cooling grass and deep in her dream she fell into a most rejuvenating sleep, where Granny's words wrapped around her like a familiar warm blanket.

'Receiving well is as good as giving the best gift.'

When she was having her morning coffee the doorbell rang, and a man with warm eyes looked down at her.

'I'm in need of something to do. I'm a landscape gardener and out of work until after the pandemic. My back garden faces on to yours. I can see you have a very sad garden and a young boy and I was wondering if he'd like to help me sort it out. I understand completely if you don't want to - but I just can't seem to get the thought out of my head.'

Days later she watched him cutting the hedge back, Conor his consistent little shadow - the two dark heads bent towards one another as they decided the best way forward. She marvelled at how she had let her guard down and how lovely it was to have close neighbours again.

The dreams kept coming - as real to her now as those two bringing her garden back to life. The language was changing in her dreams to the soft Irish burr of her Corkonian grandmother.

'*Mo chuisla* (You are my pulse)

Táim traochta (I'm exhausted)

Máirín (Maureen - Little Mary)

Tabhair saoirse dom! (Free me!)

Máirín den tobair - tahair cabhair dom (Little Mary of the Well, help me).'

She woke with a start, running out into the garden. Trusting the sense of urgency that led her to the one uncut part of the hedge she began to claw at it with her bare hands. Then Conor was beside her, handing her an old set of hedge–clippers. He placed them in her hands, knowing that she needed to do this. Then he found an old hacksaw and helped her hack. Unknown to herself she began humming the tune that had haunted her dreams.

'Where did you hear that?' he said.

'In my dreams.'

'Me too.' He answered as if it was the height of normality.

The first finger of sunlight was stretching lazily over the horizon when they found an old well covered in brambles and the sturdiest branches of the hedge. Máire looked down into it, a circular structure made of old red bricks! Her dream was out. With no chance of sleep, they dug the earth around making it ready for flowers. Conor lowered the ancient bucket they found in the undergrowth as they both hummed the old tune - it felt sacred, almost like they were humming a hymn.

Time passed and Conor found the little carved stone with the words 'Melusine, Water is Life'. On the back was carved 'Máirín den Tobair' (Little Mary of the Well). Máire knew in that place inside herself called faith that it had been carved by her Granny Máire, long ago, perhaps after a night full of dreams.

It was the last night Máire dreamed of Melusine, as the flowers bloomed around her well and three happy people picnicked in the beautiful garden.

Nekomata ~ Counting the Cat Tails

Nimue Brown

HE'S REACHED OLD AGE now, and there are questions about what will happen next. Old enough to be dangerous. Old enough to explode out of his gentle, domestic self into a new form with two tails, cruel magic and a hunger for human flesh. The only way to be safe from a domestically raised nekomata is to turn the old cat out of your home before it transforms.

He's seen this happen to other cats. This is the city of snow, and the winters are bitter here. If they turn you out and you do not quickly transform into a giant, flesh–eating monster cat, you will probably die. It might be easier if he knew what he was facing. How do you tell what sort of cat you really are? Is there any way to find out before it is too late?

This has been a good home. He remembers no other. In previous winters, sitting near the window and watching the snow fall was a sweetly hypnotic pleasure of an afternoon. No longer. Change is coming, he feels. Although he tries not to show it, he is aware of the eyes of the lady of the house as she watches him. There is scrutiny in her gaze, uncertainty and sorrow. There are muttered arguments between the people of his house and the atmosphere grows worse, day by day. His time may be growing short. He tries to cherish every soft moment, every tenderness. He learns not to stand on his hind legs when they are looking. Doing so certainly brings on the stares and the angry words, no matter how innocent his reason.

Each morning he checks his tail, to make sure he still has just the one. He does not wish to be a monster. This life has been good and he does not want it to end. He does not want to harm the lady of the house, and he fears being thrown out. Now, each time she reaches for him he is afraid that it will be to remove him from his lifelong home and send him out into the snow forever. If he transforms, will he be able to choose who he eats? He does not know.

Becoming a nekomata is a whispered enigma of a process, even to cats. No one comes back from the snow or the shift to tell housecats what really happens. There are only rumours and confusing ideas gleaned from the conversations of humans. He does not like the story that if he becomes as big as a human, he will be bound to kill his household and take their place.

All he can do is wait. The humans mutter. They tread heavily and bang doors. The long silences are tense. There are tears and raised voices. He knows many human words and tones, but even so, these current conversations are too fast, too overlapping and heavy with emotion. He does not know what they mean. Only that change must come. His old life is ending.

After the snow stops, the man of the house leaves. The lady of the house comes to him then and weeps into his fur. This is the end, he thinks. She holds him close and cries, and he does not even dare to purr as he waits for her to carry him to the door. Darkness descends, and still she does not evict him. She falls asleep by the window. It is cold and he stays with her to keep her warm. The man does not return.

He licks tear salt from her sleeping face and swears a solemn oath that no matter what happens, he will never harm or kill her. It is the first time he has spoken out loud and finding human words in his mouth surprises him. She opens her eyes and murmurs a promise that he will always have a home.

'It's a nasty superstition,' she says, 'and anyway, I love you.'

He rubs his head against her jaw. This pact is binding. They will not kill each other.

How many tails he will have in the morning no longer seems that important.

Otso and the Silver Child

Suzi Clark

THE GIANT FORESTS OF Lapland are a good place for brown bears. They are not such a good place to lose a child.

They had pulled the station-wagon to the side of the road to take a break on their way to Santa Land, through the Pyhä-Luosto National Park.

The family ate in the car, the coffee from the thermos steaming up the windows. All around them was the sound of melting snow, thudding down from the branches of the spruce and pine trees.

'I don't like the sandwich,' said the little girl in the back seat, squashed between her two brothers. 'It's reindeer.'

'Eat it,' said the mother wearily. 'It's a while before we get there. Poronkusema times ten. Anyway, the reindeer is already dead, darling.'

'I want to pee,' said the child, and clambered across her brother's lap.

He opened the door. 'Look out for wolves,' he said, grinning.

'Go with her,' said their father.

'No way,' said the brother, frowning because he couldn't get a signal on his gaming app. 'She'll be fine.'

'Who wants to see Santa, anyhow,' grumbled the other brother, stretching and yawning. 'There's no such thing.'

'Saila believes in Santa,' said her mother, 'and don't you spoil it for her.'

The child had already disappeared through the snow, plodding into the shadows of the towering trees.

'Go with her - there might be bears,' said the mother, frowning.

'No bears,' said the father. 'There's hardly any left and even if there are, they'll be hiber–nating by now.'

After a few minutes, the mother sighed and climbed out of the driver's seat. She stretched and yawned, peering towards the luminous green light of the forest, where the sun was barely filtering through the branches.

'Saila?' she called, hesitantly at first and then with a sense of urgency.

There was no reply.

Deep in the forest, the little girl was following a small bird. A blue throat. It trilled and hopped from branch to branch, and she followed. Under the trees, the snow was sparse and her feet crunched on the frozen pine needles. She kicked a pinecone and giggled when it hit a trunk. Then the trunk turned.

It was a brown bear. Standing taller than her father, the bear looked at Saila and she looked back.

'I'm sorry, bear,' she said. 'I didn't mean to hurt you.'

Saila looked sad. Then she said, 'They killed your friend and put him over the fireplace in the hotel. It made me cry. Are you sad, bear?'

The bear was very still. She was standing in a grove of silver birches. Suddenly she dropped onto all fours, never taking her eyes off the child. She seemed to sense that there was no danger from this small human being, standing so upright, looking at her so fearlessly.

Saila dug in her pocket. 'Here,' she said. She tossed the remains of her sandwich in front of her. 'You have it. It's not very nice. It's reindeer.'

The bear didn't move. Saila took a step backwards, just to be polite.

'It's alright, you have it,' she said, gesturing towards the sandwich.

The bear looked at the sandwich. 'Are you sure?' she said, in a rumbling voice.

'Yes, really,' said Saila and smiled.

'You are kind, child,' said the bear. She moved forward carefully and sniffed the sandwich. 'I prefer berries,' she said in her curious growling voice. 'But before the Big Sleep, all food is good.' She devoured the sandwich. 'Do you have anything else to eat?' said the bear in a low voice.

'I'm so sorry,' said Saila, 'nothing else.'

All around them, the silver birches shivered, although there was no wind.

'I must go now, bear,' said Saila. 'My mother will wonder where I am.'

'Must you go?' said the bear.

The silver birches shimmered and whispered. There was a strange light in the bear's eyes. Saila was clothed in innocence. She stood, upright and fearless, her white–blonde hair sparkled silver with frost, her breath surrounding her in a cloak of mystery.

She curtseyed to the bear. 'Goodbye, bear,' she said and she turned her back.

'That is not a good idea,' said the bear. 'You might come to harm in this deep forest. There are wolves. I shall walk you to find your mother.'

'I'm not sure I know the way back,' Saila said.

'Then I will show you,' said the bear. 'Follow your footprints and I will walk with you. You are too small to be alone.'

The great creature moved slowly towards Saila and then past her. There was a fragrance of pine and warm, wet fur. It was a strange smell but also comforting. They walked side by side, the silver child and the great bear. Soon they could hear the frantic calling of her family.

'This is where we must part,' said the bear gravely.

'What is your name?' said the little girl. 'I am Saila.'

'And I am the mother of Otso, the great bear,' said the old brown bear.

She turned on all fours, and then stood upright and walked into the forest. For one moment, she didn't look much like a bear at all. Saila watched her disappear into the shadows and then she ran out into the clearing. The car was empty, doors wide open, because her parents and her brothers were running up and down the road, calling her name into the forest.

'Here I am,' she called. The family turned disbelievingly and stared at her before they all started shouting at her, and then at one another, laughing and cheering, as if she had done something wonderful.

She had. Of course, she had. They would never believe her, she thought, just as they didn't believe in Santa Claus. But she, Saila the brave, the fearless, the silver child. She believed in the magic and so it was.

Phoenix

Jane Stemp

WHERE THE PHOENIX TRAILED its feathers, ash stirred and embers gleamed. Where it trod, its claws burned coal so deep that the fire stayed hidden for years beyond counting. When it leaped into the sky, meteor showers followed windblown on its trail. It flew until it found the tree that had been waiting for it, whose trunk was hollow and the floor of the hollow soft with centuries of dust.

The phoenix was tired. Its pinions were the colour of molten copper and the feathers of its body the colour of molten gold, but some things lay heavier on it than any metal. Two most of all: the years, and the ways of humankind. Those creatures that used light taken from other things and heat from others still, and were of so short a time themselves.

It looked up, into the face of the moon above the open hollow. Time no longer, it whispered; and the moon smiled. Then the phoenix pulled the sky round itself like a cloak, shut out both dark and light, and nestled down in the dust of leaves, first lightly, then with a warm breathing intensity that might have been any size at all, or no size, in any place and time.

The boy's name was Adham and the girl's name was Noor, and they lived with their parents in a small square house of mud and breeze–blocks up against the shell of an older, larger building, on the edge of a city of tents. The old building had been a gracious home with a garden and a stream and shady trees; the stream still flowed, bridged by the trunk of a fallen cedar, and when there were no chores to do the children played here among the shadows and the long grass. For an hour, an evening, too short a time, they breathed a softer air that held no taint of burning, under a gentler sky where flew no shapes of terror, in a kinder place that did not smell of fear.

That evening, under a sky of eggshell blue, Noor crossed the stream on the fallen cedar, and Adham came to meet her. As their hands touched, the trunk crumbled, and they landed together in a laughing heap on a cushion of bark and wood. It was sunset, and clouds above them, curled red and gold, drifted like feathers. For a while they lay there, wondering at the sky's beauty.

'I can hear music,' Noor said.

Adham listened. 'I can't hear it. But something. I can feel something.'

They sat up. For a moment they were still, then worked side by side, quiet and eager, scraping away dust and fragments, until in front of them was a hollow of scented bark. In it lay ...

'An egg,' Noor said, bending low. 'I thought there was music. But there isn't; only something like music.'

'It is blue like the sky,' Adhem said.

Noor stooped and picked it up, cupping it in her hands.

'And warm like ... I don't know what.' She lifted it to her face. 'It smells of cinnamon.'

'And cardamom and sandalwood,' Adhem said.

'Sunlight.' Noor caressed it. 'It's so old.'

'I think it's new. Or at least, young.'

They looked at each other. Adhem said, 'All ages, then.'

'All times,' Noor agreed. 'Let's take care of it.'

'I think it can take care of itself, but it would be good to have it with us.'

They went indoors together. Between Noor's palms the egg was heavy as gold, smooth as pearl. The music of it was on the edge of her hearing.

Adhem hunted in the chest where he kept his blankets and his treasures.

'Here is the sandalwood box that our father's grandfather carved his wife for a wedding gift.'

The box was wood and mother-of-pearl and carved with feathers or fronds; they could have been either.

'It was to wish her happiness.'

Noor gave him the egg, and went to her own room.

Here is the silk that our mother's grandmother embroidered for her husband as a wedding gift.' There were palm-trees and letters in swirling calligraphy. 'It was to wish him long life.'

They laid the silk in the scented box, and the egg on the silk, and set the box high on the rafter between their two rooms.

'Will it hatch?' Noor said.

'Of course it will hatch,' Adhem said. 'It has love and happiness and words and beauty. Sometimes they go away, but they return.'

Noor nodded. 'They are always there,' she said, 'even when we cannot see them. We have to give them time.'

They make time for themselves, the seed of the phoenix whispered to the scented darkness. And from love and memory they make more than time. All will be well.

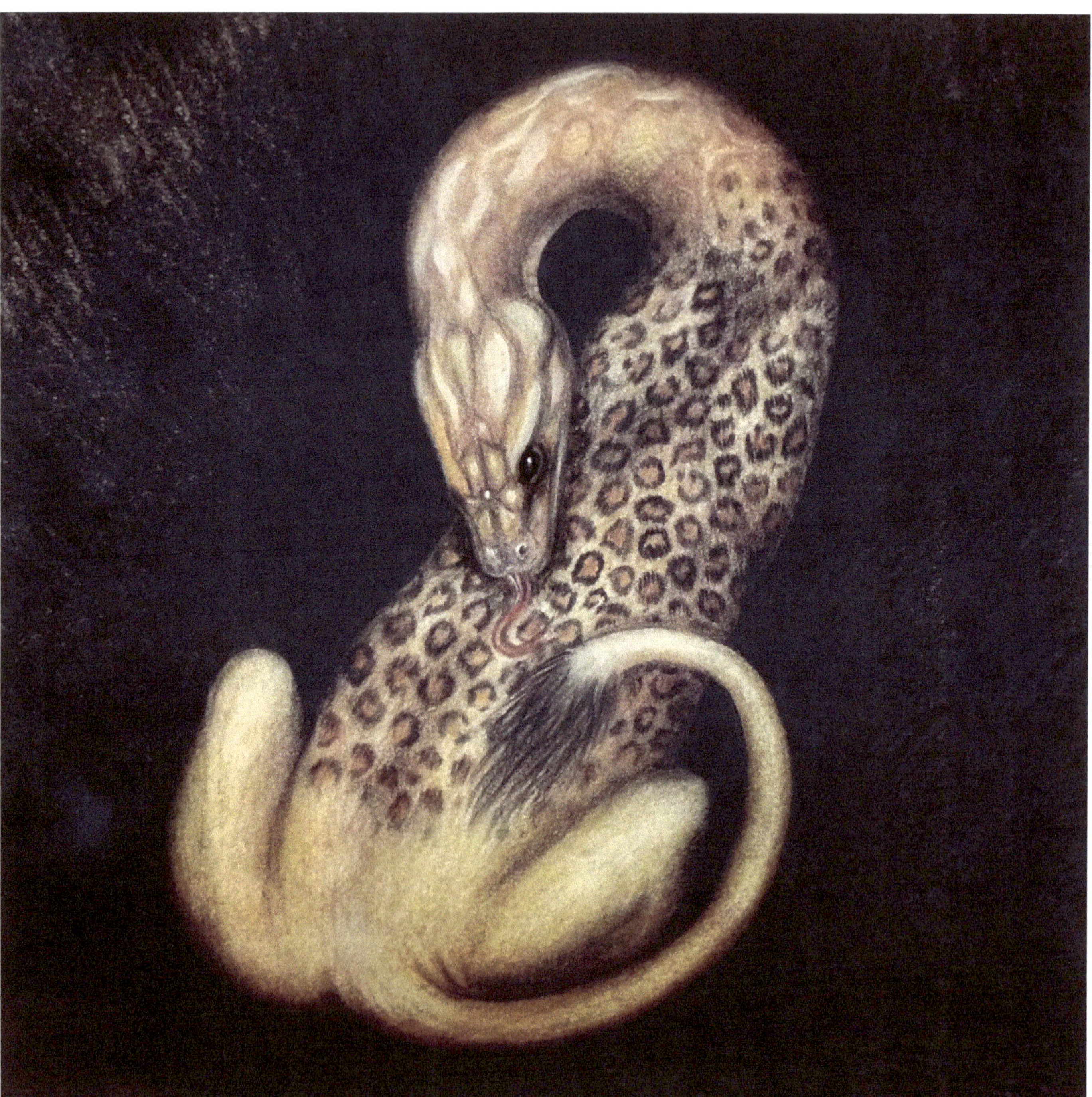

Questing Beast

Jane Stemp

ONCE IT HAD BEEN a brightness in the lens of a dewdrop, sharp as a star-dream, innocent as childhood and candle-flame. A small creature; fox-sized, hare-sized, subtle as the one and timid-eyed as the other, all quick soft movement and love, and love disdained.

Many waters cannot quench love, neither can the floods drown it; but it can fall or be cast down and turn to other things. The beast had learned that, and learned it the hard way, many years ago. It had silenced the watchdogs of its own heart, and for the sake of love it had done what should not have been done; and love had turned out to be something else. *Be wise as serpents and innocent as doves*; but the beast had gained wisdom and lost innocence. The watchdogs had been wolves after all, and no doves would come near it now.

Its body was a dapple of gold and dark and shadow, fluid as memory, strong as rage or lust. Lies had seared its tongue and soured its mouth; anger had given it strength and fear had given it swiftness. They had done the thing, the beast and the one it loved, had wrenched what they could from each other, in a world that would not give it to them. And they had found themselves sleeping with demons thereby. Did they still live, or one, or both? Together, or apart? There was no knowing.

The only certainty was that the beast could not rest. There was no sure footing or place to stand; it was afraid to go on, and afraid to stop. What lay ahead was unknown, and what followed behind was all too familiar; the armed man, metal–scaled and steel–pointed and blood–hungry, on the quest with no thought as to why or what he hunted.

There was nothing but movement, all beginnings lost and futures unravelling as the trail twisted and curved like a road in the woods, out of time and place, always here and now. The beast did not know itself anymore; whether it was the desire or the desired, the hunter or the hunted, the question or the quest. Its conscience howled in its belly, its deeds arced like lighting across intensities of craving and regret. It was its own punishment, and had borne its own vengeance.

All around the beast, the woods were bright with spring. The leaves grew early green, the birdsong fell like sunlight on rippled water. If the beast could stop, could rest, then it might be able to forget and sleep, a sleep with no ill dreams. But it could only go on, and keep going, head down, choosing not to look at what it had no share in, knowing too much about what it had left behind and what pursued it still. Crawling like a worm in the brain across the apple of the world. Knowing too much.

Until at last the skin of earth broke beneath its feet, and the beast fell into the pit that lies below the surface of things.

In a moment it gathered its haunches as if to leap, muscles tense, tail taut as whiplash. And then it looked up. Into the spring–bright air, the green wood, the lost garden. The light fell golden on fur and hide and hoof and scale.

The sky was very far away.

The sides of the pit were cliffs of shadow.

And he was there. Nothing alive to be seen of him but his eyes, a bright visored gleam below helm, above hauberk, unmoving; a reflective and impenetrable gaze. Hidden, as so many things had been. He had not been the only one. Always the many, against the one. Always the steel, against the giving flesh. Always the desire.

The beast held still. Its head was a serpent's head, armoured with scales of memory and men's fear. Its body was sleek and furred like a predator, but its feet were hooved like prey. Its eyes were the timid eyes of the hare.

If the beast looked over its right shoulder, both of them might live. If it looked over its left shoulder, one of them might die. The choice was the beast's to make.

It did not care, if only it could be left alone. It was too tired to run, or to fight, or to hide. This place was far, so very far away from hope, and the time long gone for fear.

The beast looked over its left shoulder.

Above it the steady gaze shivered into uncertainty.

There were no answers anymore. Only the quest.

Rainbow Crow

Louise Norgate

Louise Norgate

THIS ONE IS NOT *new, but a lovely reworking of a traditional tale from the first peoples of North America. The origin of the original is disputed and it may have already been adapted and changed several times but the core message of selfless sacrifice for the sake of the community remains and is more relevant now than ever.*

Long ago when the earth was still new, before the first of our ancestors walked upon its surface, it is said there came a great winter.

Snow blanketed the ground all across the earth, thick and crisp and dazzling when the sun shone. Streams, rivers and lakes froze over and icicles hung from the rocks and trees. The daylight hours were bone-cold and the nights still colder.

The earth's creatures tried to survive as best they could, but they shivered as they hunted and fed, and at night they huddled closely together for warmth, taking whatever shelter from the bitter chill they could find. But the days turned to weeks and months, the deathly grip of winter never loosened, and gradually more creatures began to perish. Trees and plants stood dormant, all was frozen, and it felt to the creatures as if the raw cold would never cease.

The creatures knew that something must be done if they were to survive, and they began to speak amongst themselves of what might bring an end to the enduring winter. They knew it was said that their Creator dwelt high above them, beyond the sky, and they said to themselves, surely if we were to beseech our Creator, They would help us? Could They not bring this terrible winter to an end?

So the creatures began to think about how they could reach their Creator. They looked at the bears, and wondered could the bears roar loudly enough, or shake the earth hard enough, for the Creator to hear? But though the bears tried, and their great paws made the earth reverberate as they bellowed out their plea, nothing came in response.

Next the creatures looked at the monkeys and said, with their acrobatics, could the monkeys climb high enough to reach the Creator? But though the monkeys tried, enough of them could never balance on each other's shoulders to reach beyond the sky.

Then the creatures said it can only be done by those of us with wings: who amongst the birds can fly up beyond the sky? And they looked at the rainbow crows, the colours of their feathers dancing like the high rainbows they sometimes saw way above, and the rainbow crows bowed their heads and agreed that they would try, though it was further than they had ever flown before.

So the rainbow crows took wing and flew upward over the snow-laden trees, climbing into the clouds and beyond. And though the atmosphere became thin and the light faded, they persevered for the longest time until suddenly they found themselves held in a strange place, luminous and still, and they heard the voice of the Creator ask them, 'Why have you come here?'

The crows told their Creator of the cruel, unceasing winter way below, and of the many creatures who had perished in its icy grip. They had come, they explained, to beseech the Creator to help: was it possible for Them to bring the winter to an end?

There was a silence until the Creator spoke again. 'I cannot end this winter for you,' They explained. 'This is a part of the cycle of the earth and it must end in its own time, though end it will. But you have travelled far to reach me, and I can give you something to ease the cold, something that can melt the ice into water for you to drink and bathe, and keep you warm even on the coldest nights. Take this now as a gift to your fellow creatures,' the Creator said, and out of the luminous air came a twig bundle before each rainbow crow, glowing with the brightest flame of fire at the end.

So the rainbow crows took the fiery twigs in their beaks and turned to fly downward, back towards the clouds and the snow-laden trees and the creatures on the earth below. Their wings were weary after such a long journey. The longer they flew the more their fiery twigs burnt down, getting closer and closer to their rainbow feathers. The smoke from the fire began to fill the air in front of each crow and their feathers began to scorch and blacken, a dark sooty coating spreading across their bodies as they flew, now exhausted, through the clouds and onward to their home.

When at last they reached the earth, all the creatures were waiting in amazement at the sight of the incoming fire carried in their beaks. As the exhausted, blackened crows landed, other creatures took the fiery twigs from their smoke-stained beaks, gathered more wood and lit fires to warm them all. Next to the flames, snow melted and small pools were thawed so that the crows might bathe and drink freely.

Now as the crows came to tell the story of what the Creator had given them, all the creatures heard how even after drinking, the smoke had hoarsened their throats and turned the crows' once-clear voices into a croak. And even after bathing, their feathers remained the deepest sooty black, the jewel-like rainbow colours now only a whisper of faint iridescence if they caught the light.

And it is said from that day forward, the creatures of the earth - and later, the ancestors who walked upon it - would look upon the blackness of the crows, hearing their hoarse calls, and remember the sacrifice they made in order to bring fire that all might survive even the coldest of winters.

Selkie and the Moon

Tom Muir

THIS BEAUTIFUL STORY WAS actually written before I drew the Selkie picture and is a deeply personal one for Tom, which makes it all the more special that it fits the illustration so perfectly.

Earlier this year I wrapped up my little Selkie drawing and sent her all the way to Orkney where she now lives. Gifted by Tom to his wife Rhonda. I love to think of her there.

There was once a seal who lived in the sea - a big, round, fat seal with whiskers, who loved to chase the fish that she fed on. She looked like any other seal, only sometimes things are not what they appear to be. For on the nights when the moon is magic, the seal would come ashore on the pink sands between the soaring red cliffs, and she would slip off her seal skin, just like taking off a dress, and she would become a beautiful woman. She would stand naked on the shore and thank the moon for the blessings that she had bestowed in allowing her to be the other half of her true nature. The moon would smile down on her, scattering her silver stardust over the selkie woman as a blessing. Then the selkie woman, lithe and slender in her human form, would dance for joy on the sand, bathed by the silvery light. And so it was for a long time.

One night as the selkie woman danced, she was observed by a human man - a farmer who lived by the shore. He saw her step out of her skin, and he stole it before she knew he was there. She wept and begged him to return her skin, but all he could see was her naked perfection, and his blood stirred. It wasn't love that drove his actions, but lust and the desire to possess this beauty all for himself. He didn't care about her pleas and tears; he wanted to own her. So he forced her to follow him home. He locked her up while he took her skin to one of his fields and he buried it deep underground. She had no choice but to stay and be his wife.

The farmer did not treat her well. He made her work hard for the scraps that he gave her to eat. She was mostly naked; he merely clothed her in tattered rags with an apron over the top. She looked like a beggar, although the farm was prosperous enough. At night, she would slip outside and beg the moon to help her return to the sea, but the moon no longer recognized her, dressed in rags as she was. And so the moon said nothing.

Sometimes in bed the farmer made her do things that she didn't want to. That is how it happened. Life sprung forth in her womb and she carried her unlooked-for burden for nine months. When the child was born, she wept. The little girl, clinging to her mother, was so like her that it was hard to believe. She was the image of her mother, only smaller. The selkie woman loved her daughter like a wilting flower loves the rain. She showered the lass with love and kisses. Her disappointed father was not so loving - he had wanted a son to help him with the farm work. What was a daughter but another mouth to feed?

The years went by and it came to the time when the farmer needed to plough the field in which he had hidden the skin. One night, under the cover of darkness, the farmer slipped out of the house and took a spade to the field to dig up the seal skin. But what to do with it? Could he risk burying it again, or was that unsafe? If the skin was under the earth or in the sea, would it eventually rot away? If it did, what would become of his beautiful wife? Would she too wither and die? He decided to hide it under the sheaves in the barn, which were ready to be thrashed, until he could find the perfect hiding place. He placed the skin under the sheaves and went back to his bed.

The following day as the farmer brought out his horse to plough the field, the little girl went to play in the barn. Under the sheaves she found a treasure - a beautiful thing of silver with dark patches on it. What could it be? To the little girl there was something familiar about it, but she couldn't think where she might have seen it before. She knew that her mother would know, so she took it to her to ask about the strange covering.

When the selkie woman saw her skin she cried out with joy. Gently she took the skin from her daughter's hands and prepared to leave. She put out the fire to protect her little girl from harm. She kissed her and told her that she loved her. Then she ran out of the house and down to the shore. Leaving her little girl was hard - the hardest thing in the world - but the selkie could not refuse the call of the sea. The sea was the other side of her true nature, and she longed for it fiercely.

Trembling, the woman took off her rags and stood naked on the pink sand so that the moon would recognize her once more. Although it was a spring morning, the moon was still lingering in the sky. She recognized the selkie woman once more and smiled to her. The selkie woman pulled on her skin and slipped quietly into the sea once again. The feel of the waves pushing against her round, fat body felt so good after years on land. The taste of freshly caught fish was magical compared to the dry bannocks the farmer gave her. She was home … she was free.

When the farmer returned from the field and saw that his wife was gone, he was furious. Not understanding what had happened, the little girl told her father of the treasure that she had found under the sheaves in the barn and how she had taken it to her mother. The farmer was enraged - he grabbed the child, put her over his knee and spanked her long and hard. She cried out in pain and fear, calling to her mother to help her.

Down by the shore, the selkie woman heard her child being beaten and she wept along with her little girl. The cries were too much for her to bear. She swam away - far away. She never stopped until she reached Sule Skerry, where the King of the Selkie Folk lived. She went to see him and, weeping, she told him about the farmer and his cruelty, and of her daughter's suffering at his hands. The king gave her a gift - one that only he could give - and she swam away with it.

That night, the selkie came to the shore and crawled up the pink sand of the beach. She stepped out of her skin and stood naked before the moon. She asked for the blessing of the moon, and was given it. The silvery beams danced around her. Carefully she hid her seal skin in a place that only she would find it and then crept silently up to the house. All was dark and quiet. The man lay asleep in his bed, while the little girl lay silently, too afraid to make a sound as the tears streamed down her face. The selkie woman was as quiet as a cat as she opened the door and slipped inside the house. She went to her daughter's bed and put her hand over her mouth to make sure that she didn't cry out and wake the farmer. The little girl, wide-eyed with wonder and joy, made no sound as the two of them crept past the sleeping man and hurried outside.

They ran down to the shore as quickly as they could, the selkie woman carrying the child when her short legs grew tired. The pink sand felt cold but soothing under their bare feet. The selkie woman slipped off her daughter's ragged nightdress and they both stood naked on the shore. She pointed up to the sky; there was the moon, shining more brightly than the little girl had ever seen before.

The selkie woman spoke: 'Mother Moon - this is my daughter. She has suffered on the land at the hands of her father. She has a grandmother and grandfather under the waves, and we will go to them now. Bless her as you have blessed me, I beseech you, oh my Mother Moon. Recognize my child.'

The moon smiled down on them both and scattered stardust over them. It glittered like silver on their white skin. The selkie mother brought out her skin, along with the gift that she had received from the King of the Selkies - a little white seal skin. She woman helped her daughter put on the skin and then slipped on her own. The two selkies slid quietly into the surging waves that were caressing the pink sand. Weightless now, they rolled and tumbled in the sea, laughing with joy that neither of them had known before. New life stretched before mother and daughter like an uncharted ocean, full of promise.

Overhead, the moon smiled a blessing on them, scattering a silver light over the water to safely guide their way.

Tiangou ~ the Story of Chang Er

Suzi Clark

CHANG ER WAS AN ordinary sort of woman, on an ordinary evening, in an ordinary village near Cheong Chin, on the banks of the Yangtse Chiang.

Her husband Hou Yi was an archer with the emperor's troop, and was often away from home, leaving her to tend the vegetable patch, wash the cotton sheets, collect firewood to take the chill off the evening mist and sing her sorrow to the lonely moon.

She was sorrowful because she could not have children, and she knew that it would complete her husband's happiness if she could present him with a son. A fat, happy son. Although, to trick the gods, she would say modestly, 'Oh, no, he is an ugly baby … nothing to look at, scrawny and always wailing.' Just to trick the gods.

At forty-five, this gift had been denied.

But she knew how much her husband loved her. He had even sent her the pelt of a white fox, wrapped in thin scarlet silk, so that it looked as though the blood of the animal spilled out over her bamboo table.

'To keep you safe, and protect you from robbers, my darling wife,' said the note written by the Mandarin. Chang Er knew this because she had taken the note to the market to have it read to her.

But the red silk disturbed her. Instead of peace and tranquillity, the white pelt with the hole where the arrow had pierced its heart, made her feel sad. So she laid it not around her shoulders but outside the front door, to propitiate the gods.

That night, she heard a howling outside the door. She opened it and there, standing on the fox pelt was a large black dog. It looked hungry, and it had its front paw in the air. She looked at the dog and the dog looked back. She could see where a thorn had gone into the pad of its paw, from the blood dripping on to the white fur.

Although Chang Er had never had a dog, she was curious. She felt a stirring of compassion, so she let the animal into her home. She poured cool water into a porcelain tea bowl and put it down. The dog sniffed the water and then lapped it up. She put some left over rice noodles on a bamboo mat. The dog sniffed them and then delicately licked them up, one at a time. The little slivers of chicken seemed to please the dog. When the mat was empty, it turned towards her and put its paw in her lap. Gingerly, afraid of being bitten, she patted the black head and then, in one swift movement, she pulled the thorn out of its paw.

The dog yelped. Hobbling to the open door, it turned and looked back at her as if in reproach. From where she was sitting, it looked as though the dog disappeared into the moonlight. Perhaps it would have eaten the moon as well, she thought wistfully. She closed the door.

The next morning when she went out into the garden, she paused. There, where the scarlet silk had lain under the pelt, there was a strange plant growing. It had heavy red fruit, smaller than plums but bigger than cherries. Chang Er felt a sudden sense of lightness in her heart. She pulled off one of the fruits, bright with dew. She licked off the dew and very carefully bit into the fruit. It was filled with tiny yellow pips. The juice was delicious. It trickled down her chin and she giggled.

And then she felt a strange sensation in her belly, not like poison, not like fear, but like life. She looked up and down the garden path. Her beloved Hou Yi was striding towards her, his face alight with laughter, his bow slung over his shoulders. In his arms he was carrying the white pelt. It was muddy and wet.

'Look what I found in the vegetable patch!' he said to his wife. 'Did it not please you, wife?'

'Oh, yes,' she said meekly. Then she patted her belly again, and felt the sensation once again. She cradled her hand around the curve. It felt full and round as a harvest moon. 'And I have some news that will please you, too.'

For a moment, in the corner of her eye, she felt sure she saw the fleeting shadow of a black dog dipping behind the weeping willow tree. Tiangou, she thought. Sometimes the blackest of spirits bring the greatest of gifts in return for a simple kindness.

Unicorns

Bill Caddick

'Take your grief and make of it a song of love' - Tuareg proverb

I didn't give my Unicorn to any of the wonderful writers that have written for my Myths in Isolation series. Because there is no story, no song, no words that can be assembled on a page that can express everything I feel about him as well as this song does.

When Bill and I first met I already had a small collection of Unicorns and drawings I had made from almost as long as I had been able to wield a pencil. As I sit here I can see Unicorns gazing down from shelves and running through glass ... and I have one hung around my neck. They are always with me. And so is this song.

Every single time Bill sang this song I cried, it's impact never lessened for me. I still weep for the wild and dirty world.

But the beauty is not lost, not if we remember to look.

I miss you Bill. I always will.

We were travelling north to sing and play

For friends that we had never met

Been working hard and didn't speak

The sky was grey and threatened wet

And I dreamed that I saw unicorns

Dreamed I saw them wild and white

Their sudden beauty lit the world

Like a star will light a winter's night

Pure as love with manes of milk

They danced and pranced and cried aloud

Bright as rainbows round the stars

Their eyes were soft and sad and proud

And I wept for the wild and dirty world

To which this beauty now was lost

And cursed the hungry mind of man

That feeds the future at such cost

My head was bowed, my eyes were closed

When in my ears their voices rang

And these few words lodged deep inside

And in my very soul they sang

We never went away

You always knew that we were near

Remember how to look for us

You'll see we were always here

I raised my eyes to seek them out

The world was empty all around

And rain came tumbling from the sky

To drown all dreams upon the ground

And when they asked me why I wept

Like one who for his dead love mourns

The only answer I could give

I dreamed that there were unicorns

We never went away

You always knew that we were near

Remember how to look for us

You'll see we were always here.

Vampire

Louise Gabriel

THIS STORY WAS WRITTEN during those uncertain and sometimes fevered days of the first lockdown in 2020 by Louise, a friend I first met in my art college days. It already feels like a little snapshot of a time so many of us felt othered and isolated in an alien new world ... it is probably the only story in the book that references the pandemic so directly and expresses the everyday oddness of the experience we all shared - even those of us who aren't vampires.

The fridge was threadbare and the freezer was empty, so she would have to make a visit to one of the few outlets still operating. Alice would have preferred to shop out of town at one or other of the farm places, specialising in locally sourced foodstuffs, she liked to alternate, their wares being different, along with the scenery, a bit of a drive, but so be it.

Alice was being careful, more so than normal, in her oversized sunglasses and alarming hat. She hated supermarket shopping, any shopping, politically, personally and now FFS she had to do it within the recently limited hours.

She was relieved by the designated distances, indicated by yellow and black tape, lashed together shopping trolleys and hastily spray-painted arrows. The smell of people was now distanced, along with their banal, unwanted conversations. The list was very short, her recipes simple, damn this hot sun and the shuffle shuffle forward. There was some idiot across the way wearing bunny ears, a nod to the Easter celebration no one was having. Twat! Anyway, she had her book, another mask, another barrier. Actually, it was an absorbing read about the human need to supplant hunting with shopping … well it was wittily written. The arrows shuffled by.

At last she was granted entry and Alice walked into the once vaguely familiar supermarket. There were more restrictions and a one-way system. Alice had to make some amusing distanced manoeuvres, almost waltzing, between the gruff security man at the door and her desired destination, the only aisle that mattered, or counted, to her.

She called her diet 'vegetarian' but no onlooker would have thought her trolley suggested that choice. Meat. Red, Red, Meat. No chicken or dull eyed fish. Liver. Steak. Maybe some lamb.

A hasty, but delayed, detour back to the pharmacy aisle for iron tablets and a few B vitamin supplements. Alice was the Queen of Nutrition, self-educated, a keen eye for the reported life-style deficiencies, she knew what she needed.

That's where he was, Mr Bunny Ears, while Alice was looking over and along the shelves, almost blindly, bloody generic labelling! Standing right next to her, despite the advice, so close she could smell yesterdays' beer. Leerily close. Alice retched discreetly, the toilets were nearby and she felt an impulse to run. He made some lame joke about paracetamol, waiting for Alice to collapse into delighted laughter but she blinked and missed it, fumbling with her hand sanitiser but that's when it occurred to her … perhaps, a different strategy? A look upwards confirmed there were no cameras. A sly glance downwards confirmed his interest. Aside from the stale beer there was a whiff of pheromones and something more deeply persuasive. Alice blinked and recalibrated. It had been so long, her mouth tasted a distant memory and smiled. She opened her clear blue eyes wide, wider, drawing him in, her lips pouting, stretching, moistening, teeth glistening, poor fool, leaning forward, happily hopeful, helpless, a flirtation, sometimes human contact is so important …

Wretch

Peter Stuart Lakanen

You idiots.

I can make words now. You're dead already. You're simply too lost in yourselves to realize it.

So much of who you are comes from instincts and understandings that don't simply predate your civilizations, they predate when you left the trees, when you were small, furry things. So much of what makes you human was not originally human. Not your fears. Not your joys.

But I … I am from your pantheon of uniquely human concepts. The first time you separated yourself from the night with a campfire and from the wild with a hut, you created the seed of me. When your ignorance brought pestilence upon your villages and towns, I visited you, hiding in your homes. Over the last ten thousand years, the more you have longed to return to the raw, to the wild, to the trees, the more that energy has moulded me, brought me into being, with increasingly greater distinction. The Black Death was the earliest I remember having a sense of whatever I am. Before that was an unending smear of sadness and longing.

Now I have returned with an intensity not felt for a hundred years. It was then that I learned how to properly express myself with pictures and sounds. I haunted your dreams as you yearned to leave your homes and return to the woods and the water. Some of the greatest art and music and creations of the twentieth century were spawned by the dreams I gave you. Not to mention the nightmares.

This time I am appearing in the least threatening of perhaps any of my forms: words on a page. That's it. I am, in this moment, inhabiting the letters, the ink, the pixels. I am *right here.* Listen to me. Because the next time I come around, I'll be combining image and sound, word and form, to appear before you in a more substantial manner. Even I don't know exactly what that will look like. This is my journey as much as yours.

The Wretch. That is what you call me. Most of what comes out of your mouths is about yourselves. You … The Wretched. The Doomed. The Ignorant Dead.

You have poisoned your world, your planet, your home. Soon enough you will long for the inconveniences of lockdown or quarantine. Your insects are dying. I can't tell which you're doing quicker to your oceans: emptying them or poisoning them.

Ice that was supposed to remain solid for millennia is gone. Gone. Ice is a safe. It keeps things locked up. You are releasing methane and pathogens and revealing artifacts that were never meant to be seen again.

You have been warned. You warned yourselves. You *know*. You all know deep down, or you think you do. You have no idea what's ahead.

Over twenty years ago, Terrence McKenna warned you that if the artist cannot find the way, then the way cannot be found. Maybe pay attention to the artists working in the liminal spaces of your world, on those boundaries within themselves, within each of you, those boundaries that have been uncomfortably close, nearer than ever for over a year now, the cost of isolation. How you haunt yourselves, forever asleep in ignorance of your potential.

Katherine saw a facet of me, and she is sharing it with you here. Do you see what she's depicted? I'm going to have to spell it out for you, simple and direct, because I can't maintain this form for long. Maybe another page or so.

Take Mother Nature and ruin her. It's not just that you've inverted her to a masculine form. You've taken a symbol of healthy, bountiful feminine energy, who provides and provides for the entire ecosystem of *your* planet, and you've reduced her to a weak and scrawny man who doesn't even have the head of a man! He is hungry and gaunt and forever torn between his humanity and his animal instincts because you starved him. And *still* you deny him, so that he remains unhealed, immature and primitive.

He is you. You are hungry, starving yourselves of your connection to the wild as you huddle in your homes because you can't remember a hundred-year-old lesson that cost you tens of millions of lives.

Katherine is holding up a mirror.

Sooner than you expect, I will return in a form that her image only hints at. Listen to your artists and their warnings and their visions. You are capable of drastic actions, and drastic measures are the only thing that will prevent billions of dead or, at the end of it all, your extinction.

I will see you again. Not as words on a page. You will see me in a truer form, and I shall arrive as a dirge when your eyes finally open, truths revealed, and I will find you mourning and bargaining for the world you threw away.

I will hold the mirror. I will be the mirror.

And you will not sleep.

Xochiquetzal

Ursula Jeffries

'WHO IS XOCHIQUETZAL?' THE young hummingbird asked his mother.

'Now who have you been talking to? You should be concentrating on plumping up now that your bright throat feathers are growing.'

'I overheard the bees saying she has been seen in the forest.'

'The bees! You stick to your flowers and leave them to theirs.'

'But they thought it was a sign of change to come.'

'She is just a memory from the old days. That was a time of many gods and goddesses. We are still here but our world is very small and we don't look outside if we have any sense. We are solitary creatures.'

Despite his mother's advice, the young hummingbird went a little further than usual in his search for nectar. Suddenly he saw a figure in the trees - a bit like the few humans he had seen in his short life but so different in the way she moved. She was singing and laughing as she lightly touched the flowers and danced through the branches. Her arms rang with golden bangles and her hair glowed with bright feathers which he recognised as coming from quetzal birds. How did she come by them? He hovered nervously, he wished he could sing with her but his voice was a raw croak and would never be melodious.

'Have no fear, little bird. Come, sit on my hand.'

She stretched out her golden-brown arm so that he could perch on her fingers.

'How lovely to see you. It helps me remember when the little children dressed as insects and birds and brought flowers for me. How I miss them all. You must have a heart of courage to hover here. They used to say your kind were reborn warriors.'

He jumped at the word 'heart'. He had heard that the old gods liked to have them as a sacrifice. She laughed.

'Don't worry, I won't need your tiny little heart. Yes, we are called cruel but so were the invaders. They took all our hearts. Where are the Aztecs now? If you give me just one of your new purple feathers, I will tell you a great secret.'

'Is that why you have come? To bring us wisdom?'

'Wisdom is a big word and means many things. My task was always to remind the people that they should live, love and laugh; enjoy the beauty around us; remember the wonders of our nature. I listened to their worries and their stories. On this visit, though, I am finding it hard to laugh and dance. It seems the only thing humanity values is gold.'

'What is gold?'

'This,' she said shaking her bangles, 'and this,' she touched the moon-shaped ornament beneath her nose. He had thought this was made of yellow feathers.

'Can you eat it?'

'No! But people must give it to buy food.'

'Why?'

'Did your mother ever say you ask too many questions?'

He felt quite faint and needed to look for nectar but he couldn't tear himself away. She was beautiful and enchanting and he could scarcely guess her powers. He waited while she hummed a little and gathered flowers, knowing it was an image he would never see again.

'I didn't intend to return. I said goodbye to this beautiful place and disappeared with my people but I have learned a terrible thing: humanity doesn't care about the bees. They have forgotten how the insects keep the plants growing and feeding the world. They are traitors and cowards.'

'What can I do?'

'You must be brave and take a message to the bees. I can offer a reward to a special human but I must leave it to the bees. I cannot stay here. You must follow your dreams. Now rest!'

In the morning the hummingbird was a little rested but very confused. It had been a night of terrible visions of ancient battles. There were shadowy figures taking feathers, wearing feathers, taking lives. The goddess had used many words he did not understand: lonely, human beings and reward were just a few. He gathered his thoughts as well as he could. After all, she had said that he and his kind were admired for being strong in the struggle of life even when alone. He puffed up his chest feathers and yawned and noticed some important things. He had two little purple feathers missing - she had indeed taken her prize - but his yawn was more than a croak. He could sing!

This new talent helped him to get the attention of the bees who soon settled round him. He gave his message as clearly as he knew how:

'The goddess returned to earth because she is lonely and worried for us all. She has seen that the beings do not care about the bees and all they care about is gold. If a being should come who ensures the future of the forest and flowers, she will reveal to them the secret of where the Aztec gold is hidden. The bees are to keep watch for such a person.'

And so it was that the bees became aware of their task. They did not understand loneliness or reward either but they would always work to keep nature reborn. The hummingbird flew away to continue his carefree life but the bees remain constantly on duty. It is said that this strange event is the cause that this part of the world is one of the few places on earth where you can find nocturnal bees. They are ferocious guards at the tops of the trees in the light of the moon; that same moon that Xochiquetzal loved in all its phases.

Yeti

Simon Heywood

I HAVE BEEN HERE a long time.

Yes, I remember the beginning.

I remember man.

I do not know where he came from.

Perhaps someone had left him to die.

He seemed to be someone a little like me,

but weaker, his limbs thin, his bones like twigs,

his bald head swollen. I did not think he would live.

He did not seem to be someone the world would ever love.

I did not love him. But he was weak, and looked as if he would die,

so I took him in, and little by little I began to teach him.

I fed him till he was strong. Then I began to show him.

Be clever, I said. The world smiles on cleverness,

but it smiles askance. Do not let the world know you are clever.

Walk humbly. Keep your eyes down to the next pace of your feet,

remember all things are alive, and all things suffer.

I taught him what to eat, and how to drink.

I told him where streams ran into the lowlands, fed by melting snow.

I taught him how to fish, how to make spears,

where to sleep, how to sing.

When I told him to take one fish, he took two.

When I told him where to hunt, he penned and herded the beasts.

When I told him to gather herbs, he made fields and gardens.

Where I told him to sleep, he built houses and streets, and lighted fires in the houses.

Where I taught him to sing, he made images of his dreams and sang his songs to them.

I took to the hills, and hid among trees and snows, and watched the firehouses growing

in the valley, every year a new house,

and I grew afraid to go into the valleys, for he would turn his spears against me,

his spears and his new songs.

And I kept to the wooded hills, until he killed trees and burned them,

and the snows began to melt,

and there was nowhere left for me.

I came down from the hills and met him in his town,

and he was surrounded by many another like him;

he had many children and grandchildren now. I said to him,

Did I not tell you

not to let the world know how clever you are? And he said,

My children must eat, and they are many.

And I said, if the snows are gone

and the rivers run dry, what will your children eat then?

And he laughed, and raged, and wept.

The women of the town led me by the hand to a place apart, and said,

You must stay here now, for if the snows are gone,

you will die without them.

And I sat in the corner of their houses; the people came to see me,

and marvelled at me, and talked long to each other about me,

and they said, This is the old one of the snows,

and the snows are melting, she has nowhere to live.

And I sat and waited.

And a small child came alone, and watched me,

and her eyes were grave, and she was still.

And at last she said,

What if all the snow melts? Where will you live?

And for a long time I did not answer her, but watched her,

until I could see who she was.

And she, too wept.

And then I took her outside and showed her the stars,

And I answered:

I never belonged in the hills and snows alone.

It was you and yours drove me into the hills.

It was you and yours who drove me into the snow.

It was not in the snow that I found your father long ago,

but he has forgotten

and you have never heard.

So now I will tell you.

I think your father has left you to die.

But you have fed till you are strong,

And now you are weeping because you think I am ending,

but I am old, I am only just beginning.

When you are grown

And your father is no more,

and the day comes when you look for me on the high hills, among dry stones where trees once grew,

and cannot find me there,

Come looking for me.

I will go now to other places.

I cannot tell you now where we may meet.

But you seem to be someone like me,

weaker, your limbs thin, your bones like twigs,

your head still a little swollen;

I know now where you have come from,

And you seem to be someone the world has loved.

Be clever, I said. The world smiles on cleverness,

but it smiles askance. Walk humbly. Do not let the world know how clever you are.

Remember all things are alive, and all things suffer.

Keep your eyes down to the next pace of your feet

And I think perhaps you will live.

And the last I saw of the town was the fires of the houses, far off in the night,

and I knew she was looking out under the stars

from the shadows between the fires.

Zlatorog

Jane Stemp

Clara shook her head.

'You don't understand.'

'I understand well enough,' Ernst said. 'You would rather have gold than flowers.'

'No. Thank you for the flowers.' Her hands were overflowing with colour. 'But they will not win you my heart, lad. It's too deep buried; and these will wither, now.'

'I didn't think of that,' he said. 'I'm sorry.'

'They will last longer when I put them in water. And I promise you, there is no fine gentleman waiting with gold to entice me.'

'And no green hunter to lead me wrong, either. But for all that, I will find Zlatorog and bring you flowers, and then -' His face brightened again. 'I promise.'

'Better not,' she said, but he was already gone.

Clara took the grey pottery jug that had belonged to her mother and filled it at the well. She had been born and raised in this cottage, and had lived there for twenty years. Then she had found her man - or he had found her - or so they had both believed, and she had gone away with him into another country.

And they had been happy, until their only child, their son, had been lost in the forest.

Love had not outlasted loss. When, a year later, her man's horse returned riderless home, there was nothing else to stay for. She had left the forest lands where pine trees clawed the air, and alders stood with their roots in dank water, and returned to this high village, bringing only what she had taken away for her dowry, and a cart to carry that, and the horse to draw the cart.

Her parents had been alive to welcome her home, and she had cared for them until the end of their lives. Now she lived alone. There was land enough round the cottage to graze a cow and a calf, and to feed a few hens, plump and feathery as pillows. She paid the rent with what they gave her, and by sewing and mending all the hours she could. There were herbs and flowers too, when the hens and beasts could be kept from eating them. Always she had loved flowers, and the first ache in the heart of her marriage had been when she could not make them flourish round the house in the dark woods far away.

Ernst had not been the first to come courting, since she returned; but Clara felt too immeasurably old for any of them, as if she had lived through years of pain. She wanted nobody, not even to share her grief with.

She set the jug back on the table and arranged the flowers in it. The clustered rainbow of their petals above the grey glaze lifted her heart, for a moment, like birdsong on a day of rain. Once upon a time, when the world and she and love were young, she and the birds had sung all day. She did not sing now, but for a moment she felt as if she could; as if the grief-hard kernel of her heart might one day make itself a pearl.

That night she left the shutters open and fell asleep counting stars.

In the morning she was outside early, loading the cart with eggs and cheese and butter. Early to market was the best time to sell, and she was in a hurry; but there on the stone beside the gate was a clump of flowers white as starlight, bedded in green turf. Ernst must have brought them, then cupped water in his hands, for droplets gleamed on the bright petals, and the dampened ground held one print of a hobnailed boot.

The water might keep all fresh until she returned; but perhaps it would not. Clara tethered the horse to the fence and picked up flowers and turf together. They quivered between her hands like some small creature, or a lost nestling; without knowing why, she stroked the white petals and murmured, 'Later; I'll be back later.' They would be safe in the kitchen, out of the sun and the wind, and when she came home she would plant them.

When she had sold everything she could, and bought all she needed, she harnessed the horse at once, and went back without letting him graze at the wayside. But she took the time to rub him down and groom him carefully before, at last, she dug out a place for the new plant.

It moved between her hands again when she picked it up; quietened when she turned towards the door; quivered when she knelt by her flowerbed. Only when she rose and turned to face the mountains did the trembling cease.

Clara so wanted those flowers in her garden; wanted their brightness and beauty.

She took the first step towards the high peaks. Then another.

The sky grew dim with twilight, the east side of every mountain dark with shadow. The path led her beside an uncanny place of stagnant water and twisted roots; the villagers said it was the green hunter's home. Shadows and reflections shaped a face with eyebrows like dark wings, and she held the flowers close. They were all light in her hands, light to hold and bright to see.

Soon there were unseen depths on one side, crags rising sharp on the other. At last, she was on the narrowest of trails between walls of rock, completely in the dark. She hesitated. How was it possible to go on?

She went on.

At last there was light.

And then there was Zlatorog.

The light came from two directions at once. The setting sun spilt it blood–red over the basalt shelf, tinting Zlatorog's breathing sides with life. The rising moon struck it from the curve of one golden horn, turning it to a crescent of silver.

Zlatorog lay, watching her. He was old; older and lonelier than she had ever felt. And he knew her pain. She saw it in his eyes.

Between them was a strip of green turf, where the mingled lights made silver and gold of the flowers, except in one ragged wound of dark. Slowly Clara knelt, and set her flowers in it. There was a moment, a movement, as if they sighed with gladness, and then the place was whole again.

Love. Loss. Letting go, however much you wanted, however much it hurt. Living, all the same.

She and Zlatorog were alone together.

Memories settled round her, like the dust of pearls.

www.ingramcontent.com/pod-product-compliance
Lightning Source LLC
Chambersburg PA
CBHW042111160726

48295CB00018B/1059